Penguin Books
Pity Him Afterwards

Donald Westlake was born in Brooklyn, New York, in
1934. His family moved to Albany where he grew up and
went to school. He attended Chaplain and Harpur Colleges
and became editor of newspapers at both colleges. He served
with the air force in Germany, worked as associate editor to
a literary agent and acted for a season.

Several of his short stories have been published; one in
Best Detective Stories of 1959. His first novel, *The
Mercenaries*, was published in 1960 and won an award from
the Mystery Writers of America. It is now available in
Penguins, as are *The Busy Body*, *Killing Time*, and *Killy*.
Mr Westlake is married and lives in New Jersey with his
wife and two sons.

Donald E. Westlake

Pity Him Afterwards

Penguin Books

Penguin Books Ltd, Harmondsworth,
Middlesex, England
Penguin Books Australia Ltd, Ringwood,
Victoria, Australia

First published by T. V. Boardman 1965
Published in Penguin Books 1970
Copyright © Donald E. Westlake, 1964

Made and printed in Great Britain by
Hunt Barnard Printing Ltd, Aylesbury
Set in Intertype Times

To Mel and Nedra

If a madman were to come into this room with a stick in his hand, no doubt we should pity the state of his mind; but our primary consideration would be to take care of ourselves. We should knock him down first, and pity him afterwards. – *Samuel Johnson*

The madman clung to the side of the hill, hidden by darkness and trees. Staring over his left shoulder he could see the lights in pairs crossing the bottom of the night, round whites when coming aslant, red dots when going. Only the circling red light atop the state police car did not move on, across the valley floor and out of sight. The ambulance had gone now, and the traffic jam had been broken up, but the state police car did not move on.

The hill face was steep here, furred with spring grass. Below was a dark mass of trees, and more trees above, but here on this steep band across the hill there was only grass. The ground was soft and moist.

It was the night of the new moon, so the stars had the cloudless sky to themselves. The madman, clinging to the side of the hill, was a darker mass against the ground. His fingers were dug into the earth and he kept looking over his left shoulder. The suitcase was on the ground beside him.

Down below him, past the trees, he could see the headlights going by. He was waiting for the state police car with the circling red light to go on, to go away with the rest of the lights, and then he could move. But the state police car didn't go away.

And now more red lights came, borne on the stream of headlights. The madman reared up, almost losing his balance and rolling down the hill, and stared in hatred at the revolving red lights. Three more of them, all stopping by the first. Dimly amid the lights he could see men moving, and then a different kind of light appeared. A small nailhole of light in the darkness. Flashlights. Men with flashlights crossed the road down there and started up the hill, spreading out, opening like a fan. He lost sight of them all in the trees, and saw *there* a flicker of light, and *there*. And *there*.

They were coming after him.

The madman put his head down on the ground, his burning forehead against the cool dampness of the turf. Despair washed over him. Just after dinner he'd broken out, and before midnight he was to be caught again. They would make him scream for this, the shock every day, death and rebirth every day, going down and away to spasmodic shrieks and coming back to twitches and deafness and the cold blue eyes of Doctor Chax. (There was no Doctor Chax; all the doctors were Doctor Chax; all the doctors had the cold blue eyes and the warm brown voices, and told him while they tortured him that the torture was for his own good; he had made up the name, Doctor Chax. It was all of them.)

Voices wafted up the hill to him on the cool air. The turf was cool against his forehead. Voices wafted up, and the blundering of men upward through the trees.

He raised his head. He stared upward, toward the top of the hill, crowned with more trees. His eyes shone just slightly in the starlight.

He would *not* go back to Doctor Chax. He would *not*.

He pulled his left leg up, and then his right. Moved his left hand forward, and then his right. On hands and knees, and then upward to his feet, leaning forward into the slant of the hill. He took three staggering steps upward, always teetering just short of falling backward down the hill toward the flickering flashlights down under the trees. Then he remembered the suitcase, still lying where he'd left it, three paces back. He shook his head heavily from side to side, grimacing and growling in exasperation, and, bent far forward, thudded his fists against the turf.

There was nothing for it but to go back. The suitcase was necessity.

He scrambled back down to the suitcase and grabbed it in his right hand. He glared quickly downslope, saw the flashlights closer, nearly to the upper limit of the trees, and growled deep in his throat. (He wouldn't talk to the doctors, and couldn't talk to the other patients, and there was no one else to talk to. He'd gotten the habit of talking to himself, but mainly silently, in his head, with only grunts and growls coming to the surface, a mannerism common among men who live alone or work alone. It was not a symptom of his madness, but of his solitude.)

He clambered up the steep slope now like a crippled spider, dragging the suitcase. He hurried as fast as he could go, panting noisily; four years of sedentary life in the asylum had left him out of shape for running.

He didn't slow down when he reached the trees above, but pulled himself upward through them, grasping at trunks and shrubbery with his left hand, jerking himself forward from hold to hold, the suitcase bumping and dragging along behind him. The ground here was less even, scored with thick roots and pocked with stones, dangerous with mulch-filled craters that gave no footing. But the slope was less steep, and he drove himself forward, stumbling and panting, pursued by Doctor Chax, who skimmed along effortlessly a yard above the ground, his long white coat trailing like a nightgown, his progress unencumbered by a heavy suitcase and the need to crawl on the surface of the earth rather than fly. But though he had the unfair advantages, and though he was just behind, he could never quite catch up.

The madman's groping left hand closed on barkless wood, above him and across his path. He made a startled noise, feeling the smooth undulant surface beneath his hand, and then grasped it tighter and pulled himself upward, his feet scrabbling at the rocky ground.

A railing. A fence, fence of some sort. It was pitch-black here, under the trees. But ahead of him was greyness, as though there were a level cleared surface beyond the fence.

The fence was made of two crossbars, one about two feet from the ground and the second another two feet higher. The madman pushed the suitcase under the lower bar, then crawled between the two bars and straightened on the other side.

He was standing on gravel. He had come up at the corner of a lookout parking area beside a small blacktop road. There was no traffic on the road and, because it was a Monday night, no cars parked by the lookout. On the weekend lovers and policemen came up here.

He felt the need to keep running, but his breath was ragged

11

and there was a sharp pain in his side. He leaned against the top railing of the fence, doubled over, trying to catch his breath and to make the pain go away, and listened for the sounds of the pursuers. But they were moving more cautiously, searching for him in crannies and behind trees, and he had outdistanced them. He couldn't even see their flashlights any more.

When the pain lessened and his breathing grew less difficult, he straightened and turned away from the railing. Carrying the suitcase, he walked across the softly crackling gravel to the blacktop road. There was a double white line up the middle of the road, a faint smear in the darkness. He stood on the white line a moment, and considered.

He had been going up. They would expect him to continue going up. So he would fool them. He would follow the road downward.

He no longer felt the same urgency. He had outdistanced them, and outfoxed them. So he walked at a normal pace down the road, keeping in the middle, walking on the double white line. There was no traffic at all.

He walked for twenty minutes and then he came to a house and a garage. There was a light on in the office of the garage – an illuminated clock, that was all – but the garage was closed. The pumps out front were dark and the floodlights at either end of the garage property were dark and the big gasoline emblem sign was dark.

The house was behind the garage, an old two-storey clapboard house, with faint lights showing in the old downstairs front windows. The people who lived in the house were probably the ones who operated the garage.

The madman crept up past the garage, toward the house. The illuminated clock on the garage office wall read five minutes after twelve. It threw the faintest of light on the madman as he moved past the window, heading toward the house. He was wearing a dark grey suit, old and wrinkled and shapeless, the coat hanging open and the sleeves too short. He wore a battered hat on his head, one he'd found in a dump by the roadside on his flight from the asylum; the hat had obviously been thrown away because it was out of style, with a brim too wide for current fashion. The suitcase he carried, which forced him

12

to walk in a lurching half-crouch, was bulky and black, fastened with leather straps. Suitcase from the driver who had given him a lift, hat from the dump, suit from the janitor's closet in the basement of the asylum.

The house was up a short slope from the road, with uneven slate steps up the slope to the porch. The slate steps were flanked by rock gardens.

The madman left the suitcase on the ground next to the porch, then climbed noiselessly up the stoop and over the porch to the nearest window. He looked in and saw a barrel-chested old man with grey hair asleep in an armchair. The armchair had maroon slipcovers with a design of great white flowers. The old man wore a dark-patterned flannel shirt with the sleeves rolled up, and grey work trousers, and black wool socks but no shoes.

There were two light sources. One was a table lamp on a drum table beside the sleeping old man, shining on the gnarled hands resting in his lap. The other was a television set across the room, showing a commercial.

The madman moved until he could see the rest of the room. The old man was alone.

The madman crouched on the porch. What to do? He needed a place of refuge, a safe hiding place just until morning. But it would have to be indoors, where the searchers wouldn't look. It would have to be inside this house.

The madman moaned low and soft, and shook his head back and forth. He felt very mournful, because human beings were so perverse, and they forced him to such excesses.

If human beings were *good*, how sweet life would be! But Doctor Chax summed them up: warm brown voice and cold blue eye. They would *act* friendly and sympathetic, but it was all false; just turn your back and they would betray you.

The madman hunkered on his heels, resting his back against the clapboard front of the house, between the door and the window. What he wished he could do was just knock on the door and say to the old man, 'Pardon me, sir, I would very much like to abide here until morning, if I may?' If only the old man would say, 'Of course! Aren't we all brothers?'

But he wouldn't.

And if he did, it would only be because he'd recognized him, as the driver did, and was planning to telephone to Doctor Chax as soon as he could sneak away.

That was the way people were.

The driver, too. He had seemed so *good*. But he had proved himself false.

The madman had been walking beside the highway. He hadn't been actively trying to hitch a ride, because he knew that was the way to draw attention to yourself and wind up with someone phoning the police: 'Suspicious-looking character thumbing a ride out on the highway.' So he'd just been walking along, in the suit and hat and sneakers – his own sneakers, the only shoes they'd let him wear at the asylum – when the car had stopped. A noisy eight-year-old Plymouth. And the driver had said, 'Want a ride to the next town?'

He had gotten in. Though for a second he had hesitated, afraid the driver would ask him questions: 'Where you headed?' 'Where you from?' But he knew himself to be clever; he'd be able to think up lies.

The asylum had done that much for him. They'd put him away there not because he was crazy – he knew what *crazy* was, and it wasn't him – but because he'd never learned to lie. All the people who thought they weren't crazy, they told lies all the time. It was the way the world was run. Big lies, little lies. He saw truth, and told truth, and so they said he was crazy and they put him away in the asylum. And in the asylum he learned the value of cleverness – how to fool them, how to lie to them –and he learned the uses of falseness. But still they wouldn't let him go. His rages were righteous and came only when he was strongly provoked, but they refused to accept that. And where he had learned to make do without truth when necessary, he would never learn – never even *try* to learn – to make do without logic and righteousness.

So, armed with the cleverness they'd taught him in the asylum, he had gotten in the car, in the Plymouth, sitting beside the driver. The driver pushed the Plymouth very fast down the highway, and pleasant soothing music came from the car radio. And the driver didn't ask questions; instead, he talked about himself.

He was an actor, he said. He was on his way to a job in a summer theatre. It was a repertory company, which would present eleven plays this summer. No packages, the actor assured him, and went on to explain that packages were touring shows, usually with a famous actor in the leading role, which went a week at one summer theatre and then a week at the next, and so on. But the summer theatre where the driver was going was not like that; it was true summer stock, with a company that put on all the plays itself, doing this week's play tonight, rehearsing next week's play this afternoon.

The driver was one of those people who loves his job so much he can never stop talking about it. He and the madman rode together nearly three hours, and the driver never stopped talking about theatre. He told the madman all about the way a summer theatre is run, and the kind of part for which he'd been hired, and what he had done in his career up till this point, and the names of all the people in theatre he knew, and anecdotes about them, and on and on. After a while, he was repeating himself. But the madman didn't mind. It was pleasant to listen to, and he was actually interested; at one time he himself had thought idly of a theatrical career. But that was in another life.

Behind and beneath the driver's rambling talk the radio played music and commercials and news broadcasts and weather reports, all soothing, soporific, a pleasant soft accompaniment to the driver's chatter. Until the eleven o'clock news broadcast, which told all about the madman, and gave his description.

The driver had known immediately. The madman could tell. But, to try to fool him, he'd said, 'Why, that description could fit anybody. It could fit me. It could even fit you.'

It was true. The driver and the madman were both approximately the same age and the same size. Their hair colouring was different and facially they looked not at all alike, but in general build and chronological age they were quite similar.

The driver was a good driver, but really a very bad actor. He would never have been a famous star, even if he'd lived. He'd let the nervousness and the false jollity show in his voice, and his true meaning had been clear when he'd said, 'I'm getting hungry, aren't you? Let's stop at the next diner for a couple hamburgers.'

Betrayers, all of them. What business was it of his, anyway? They were fellow human beings. Shouldn't they be helping one another? Why should the driver side automatically with Doctor Chax, without even giving the madman a chance to tell his side of the story?

He had been so enraged he had forgotten himself and done a foolish thing. He should have waited till they'd come to a stop, in the darkness outside some diner. But the betrayal was so base, his anger so strong, that he couldn't wait. He reached out his hands and clamped them on the driver's throat, and the Plymouth spun off the road, missing the oncoming cars, and smashed into a tree.

Still, after the foolishness he had been smart. Immediately the car had stopped, even before the flames had begun to lick up, he had grabbed the dead driver's wallet and suitcase. Then out of the car and away, into the darkness, while behind him the flames had suddenly opened like a great mouth, engulfing the car, and all at once exploding.

Some busybody must have seen him leave the car and run away up the hill. He had planned to stay there until the police had gone, and then continue on along the highway, but some busybody must have seen him run away. Another one who sided automatically with Doctor Chax.

The old man would, too. They *all* did.

The madman felt very sad, not wanting to do what he knew he would have to do. But wasn't self-preservation the prime law? He couldn't let his emotions stand in his way, shouldn't let weakness cause him to be captured and turned back to the tortures of Doctor Chax.

Hadn't his father told him, time and time again, the mark of a man is that he always does what is necessary, no matter what?

But it was hard, it was so hard ...

Moaning softly, the madman crept back down the stoop to the suitcase, and removed one of the leather straps. The strap was an inch wide, tough black leather, with a square brass buckle. He twisted it around his left hand, and went back up on the porch.

The door was locked. The two living-room windows were locked.

Sorrow began to be displaced by irritation, and irritation by anger. Wasn't the task difficult enough as it was? Did it have to be made even more difficult?

He circled the house like a winter wind, seeking some crack to come in through, and found it at last in a small kitchen window, the only unlocked window on the ground floor.

It was a job getting through. The window was high, and just inside was the kitchen sink, a broad deep old-fashioned sink against which he cracked his left elbow. He gritted his teeth with the pain, and crawled the rest of the way through the window and down across the sink to the floor, and huddled there on all fours, rubbing the elbow. His head kept moving back and forth in a distracted way, like the head of a snake. He'd lost his hat on the way in, and he found it and put it back on before going any farther. He thought of it as a kind of disguise.

The kitchen was in darkness. He left it, and moved through a dark hall to a semi-dark dining room, lit indirectly from the one lamp burning in the living room.

The old man was still asleep. The television set murmured – a man at a desk was interviewing a man on a leather chair, and both were laughing, and a crowd of unseen people were laughing – but other than that the house was silent.

The madman tiptoed across the living-room, his sneakers silent on the faded Persian-style carpet. He moved around behind the floral armchair in which the old man slept. He held the leather strap now in both hands and he dropped it over the old man's head and tightened it around the old man's neck.

The old man awoke and thrashed. But the madman had the leverage, pinning the old man back against the chair, keeping the strap tight around the old man's throat, and after a while the thrashing subsided and stopped.

The madman switched off the table lamp before moving, because he didn't want to see the old man's face. He'd seen the faces of people who'd been strangled, and it always made him feel sick. The television set gave wan blue light.

In the near-darkness he crossed the room. He had seen the staircase while the light was on, and he headed straight for it and felt along the wall till he found a light switch. It shouldn't frighten anyone if the staircase light went on; those upstairs would think it was the old man, coming up to bed.

He clicked the switch on, and a light blossomed at the head of the stairs. He climbed the stairs quickly – they were covered in grey carpet, badly worn in the centre – and paused in the small second-floor hall.

There were four doors, two shut and two open. He investigated.

One of the open doors led to the bathroom. The other led to a bedroom with a double bed in it. But there was no one in the bed.

He opened the closed door on the right, and found the old man's wife asleep. She, too, woke up, just as the old man had, but her struggles were never as strong as his had been.

The closed door on the left led to a nursery, with a crib. But the crib was empty.

The madman was glad. He would have hated it if the crib had had an occupant.

But that was the full household. The old man and his wife, a married son or daughter and mate, and a grandchild. The younger couple and the grandchild must be away visiting. The madman was glad of it.

Though sometimes he thought the best thing would be to kill all the children. Then the human race would stop. But it was too much for one man to do. Though when he tried to argue with himself that children were for the most part better than adults – more honest, more willing to let a man alone, more apt to see truth – he could always counter the argument with the reminder that children, unless they are stopped, grow into adults.

He went back downstairs. The upstairs hall light let him see fairly well in the living-room, well enough to go get the old man and tumble him out of the chair and drag him by the armpits across the room. He dragged the old man upstairs – a job that

winded him again – and dumped him on the floor in the bedroom with his wife, and closed the door. Then he went back
downstairs, switched on living-room lights, switched off the
upstairs hall light, and unlocked the front door. He went outside and got the suitcase and brought it in with him, and locked
the door again. Then he pulled the living-room shades, turned
off the television set, and opened the suitcase on the floor.

He was safe now. Safe for tonight in this house. Safe for
tomorrow with the contents of the suitcase. Shirts, socks, shoes,
slacks, and a blue-grey suit. He could dress properly, and
shave himself, and make himself presentable, and then he could
go anywhere.

But go where?

He sat cross-legged on the floor, in front of the suitcase, and
frowned as he tried to find an answer. All of his plans till now
had been aimed at getting away from the asylum. He hadn't
thought of what to do next, what to do once he was safely free.

What could he do? Where could he go?

He couldn't go home. He couldn't go anywhere near home.
But where else was there? He remembered enough about the
outside world to know it was a world of papers and numbers.
If he tried to get a job anywhere he would have to have a
Social Security card, and they'd want a list of former employers,
and they'd want to know if he was in the Army . . .

He sat cross-legged on the floor and looked at the suitcase,
and tried to think what he would do tomorrow. He was on
his own. No one would help him. He was alone, with the whole
world ranged against him, all of them waiting for a chance to
turn him over to Doctor Chax.

Maybe, if he could get out of the country, get to Mexico or
Canada . . .

How much money did he have?

He pulled out the wallet he'd taken from the driver, and
found it contained forty-three dollars. Not enough, forty-three
dollars. He'd have to find more.

Maybe there was some money here in the house. Or he could
find the old man's keys and get into the garage, and get the
money out of the cash register.

He put the forty-three dollars back in the wallet, and then he stopped, and looked hard at the wallet.

The wallet had more than money in it. The wallet had cards in it, all sorts of identification cards, in four plastic pockets.

He dragged all the cards out and read them, read every word. Studied them, turned them over, shuffled them back and forth in his hands. And he began to smile.

There was a driver's licence.

And a membership card in Actor's Equity.

And a laminated reduced photostat of an Army discharge.

And a Social Security card.

He looked at the cards for a long while, and then he set them down gently on the floor, all in a row, and put the wallet down beside them, and he made a careful search of the suitcase.

There were only two things of interest in the suitcase, two large manila envelopes. In one of them were four letters, the sum total of the correspondence between the dead driver and the producer of the summer theatre, in which the driver had been hired for the summer season. And in the other was a batch of glossy large black-and-white photographs of the dead driver in an actorish pose, arms crossed and head tilted, looking very dramatic, with dramatic lighting effects in the background. Scotch-taped to the back of each photo was a mimeographed résumé of the dead driver's theatrical career.

The madman smiled and laughed and nodded his head, and affectionately patted the cheek in the photographs, because all at once he knew what he would do. He would take the dead driver's place. He would go on to that summer theatre, and he would be safe there until the end of August, and then he would decide what to do next.

Could it be done?

The madman cocked his head to one side, and touched a fingertip to his chin. Sitting cross-legged amid the dead driver's effects, a faint smile on his face, he looked like a child beneath the tree on Christmas morning, having been asked by a kindly uncle with which toy he intends to play first, and trying pleasurably to decide on an answer.

And could it be done?

He thought back to things the driver had told him: This was the driver's first season at this particular summer theatre. He knew no one else who'd been hired, nor did he know the producer.

But there would be a photograph. One of the glossy photographs with the résumé on the back. The driver would have sent it when he applied for the job.

The madman sucked on his lower lip between his teeth, and squinted at the darkness in the dining-room archway. Could he be clever? Could he overcome the problem of the picture?

What if it was the wrong picture?

'Why, I must have sent you the wrong picture,' the madman said aloud, smiling. 'That's my room-mate's picture. We were both sending out pictures at the same time and I must have sent you his picture by mistake.'

Was that possible? Yes, of course, but would it be believed?

What if he got more pictures like it? Tomorrow morning he could go down to the nearest city and go to a photographer, and have the photographer take pictures of himself in the same style as these pictures of the dead driver. Then he could switch the résumés to the new pictures, and give one of them to the producer to take the place of the wrong picture in his files.

If he had legitimate-looking pictures, and all the right cards, wouldn't they have to believe him? They wouldn't even consider the possibility that he wasn't what he seemed.

Unless they already knew the driver was dead.

Would they know that? The summer theatre was over four hundred miles from here, in another state. The dead man's home was three hundred miles in the opposite direction, and in a different state altogether.

Besides, it would take them a while to find out who the driver was. The car was all blown up, and the madman had the driver's identification papers.

But it would mean that he would have to act, have to be in plays all summer. Could he do that? He didn't have any experience in that at all.

But he did have a good memory, an excellent memory. There was a heightened clarity in his mind, because not all of it was

21

functioning, and so the part that was working had more concentrated power. He had a really magnificent short-range memory. He tended to forget things after a month or two, forgetting much more completely than a normal mind, but to the same extent he remembered recent things with more sharpness and detail than a normal mind.

So he wouldn't have trouble learning parts in plays. And he could remember a lot of what the driver had told him about himself.

But would he be able to act well enough to fool them? Could he convince them he was an actor?

Well, wasn't acting simply being clever? He had consciously trained himself in being clever. Surely he was more clever than the driver had been, because he had seen the driver's intentions at once but the driver hadn't known he knew until it was too late.

He nodded to himself. He would at least try it. At the worst, they would decide he was a bad actor and they would fire him. There was no real risk of exposure, if only he remembered to be clever, to lie and make believe and fool them.

The driver had told him he was due at the theatre on Wednesday. This was Monday night. So he had all day tomorrow to get the pictures taken and to think about his plan and see if there were any problems he'd overlooked.

But now his original idea had to be changed. He couldn't stay here till morning. He had to leave as soon as possible, and be in the city by morning, so he could find a photographer.

He scrambled to his feet, closed the suitcase, and carried it upstairs with him. He went into the bathroom and stripped and took a quick hot shower and then dressed again, in the driver's clothes. The shirt and suit coat fit perfectly, but the trousers were too tight around the waist. He left the button open, with the belt concealing the V opening. The shoes were too large, but that was all right. A lot better than being too small.

When he was washed and shaved and dressed, he closed the suitcase again, left it in the hall, and went into the bedroom where the bodies were. He found the key ring in the old man's right-hand pants pocket, and then carried the suitcase downstairs. He picked up the wallet and cards, put them all together again, and stowed the wallet in his hip pocket. Then he looked at the old man's keys, and smiled happily when he saw the silver key with GM on it. An automobile ignition key. Still smiling, he left the house.

He found the car, a five-year-old Chevrolet, parked beside the garage. He dropped the suitcase on the back seat and slid behind the steering wheel.

It had an automatic gearshift, which was a good thing. It had been a long, long time since he had driven a car, and most of his knowledge of driving had faded with the rest of his older memories. But with an automatic gearshift, he would be all right.

Nevertheless, he drove very jerkily at first, and it was a good thing there weren't any other cars on the road. It took him about ten minutes to get used to the accelerator and brake, but finally he got the car under control.

Once the car was running the way it was supposed to, he had leisure to remember that he had neglected to get the money from the garage cash register. He got angry at himself for that, and pounded his fist on the steering wheel. But he didn't want to go back. The forty-three dollars would have to last him. When it was gone, he could always get some more.

The narrow blacktop road wound among the hills for a long time, and finally deposited him in a small town where he found a turn-off that took him to a divided highway, the same one he'd been on before. The place where he'd killed the actor was about fifteen miles back the other way.

He drove all night, too excited to feel tired, and at eight-thirty in the morning he came to a medium-sized city and found a photographer's shop, where the owner was just opening for business. He went in, carrying one of the dead man's pictures, and said, 'Can you make me some pictures just like that?'

The photographer looked at the picture and said, 'Sure. You an actor?'

'Yes. How fast can you make them?'

'I should be able to have them ready by Thursday.'

'Oh, no! This morning.'

'This morning? Listen, I've got too many rush orders as

it is. I've got a one-man operation here, my friend, and I – '

'But I need them this morning.'

Then the photographer looked sly. The madman saw it, and felt the anger rising in him, but forced it down out of sight. The photographer said, 'A real hurry job like that, my friend, that'll cost you.'

'How much?'

'How many copies you want?'

'Ten.'

'Fifty dollars.'

'All right,' said the madman, knowing then he would have to kill the photographer. For being sly, and unfriendly, and unwilling to help his fellow man for the simple reason that we are all human beings together. Even if he'd had enough money to pay the photographer, he would still have had to kill him.

He posed in the same position as the dead actor in the other picture, and the photographer gave him the same kind of dramatic lighting. Then the photographer told him to come back in three hours, and he went away and had a big breakfast of pancakes and coffee, and took a nap in the car, which was parked on a residential side street. A small boy awoke him at eleven o'clock by banging on the fender of the car with a stick, and he got out of the car and took the stick away from the boy. He had the boy's shoulder in his left hand, the stick in his right hand, and the anger was building in him, but then he saw two women with shopping carts walking toward him, and he knew he didn't want to have to run away until he got the pictures, so he let the boy go.

The photographer had the pictures ready when he got back, and they weren't as good as the other ones had been, but they would do. He and the photographer were alone in the shop, so when the photographer asked for his fifty dollars the madman jumped on him. He'd forgotten to bring a rock or any kind of weapon with him, but he managed to break the photographer's left elbow-joint very early in the fighting, and that drained the photographer of strength, and then it was simple to strangle him.

He went back to the car and looked around, but the boy

was nowhere to be seen, and there wasn't time to look for him. He got into the car and stowed the new pictures in the suitcase and drove to the bus depot and left the car in a parking lot across the street. The attendant gave him a yellow ticket stub with red numbers on it. He carried the suitcase and ticket stub across the street with him and then threw the ticket stub away. He knew about licence numbers and automobile descriptions, and he knew it would be dangerous to drive that car any farther.

He bought a ticket to Cartier Isle, which was where the summer theatre was. He had a four-hour wait this time, so he checked the suitcase and went to a movie. He fell asleep in the movie house and got back to the bus depot just in time to get his suitcase and climb on the bus.

Mel Daniels came into Cartier Isle on the Thursday afternoon bus, twenty-four hours late for work. He'd shaved and made himself presentable, but he still had the shakes and a grinding headache. Mel Daniels and his Magic Hangover.

The bus rolled down the main street to the middle of town, and came to a stop in front of the depot, which was also a drug store, lunch counter, and news-stand. End of the line. Mel and the other four passengers climbed down to the sun-bright sidewalk, carrying their luggage. Mel had his father's suitcase, the remnant of a matched set.

He stood squinting on the sidewalk a minute. There wasn't a cloud in the sky. The sun was bright enough for him to be on Mercury by mistake. He put his free hand over his eyes and hurried on into the relative dimness of the store.

A little bald man in a white coat stood behind the tobacco counter to the left. Mel went over and said, 'Can you point me at the summer theatre?'

'Other side of the lake.'

'Other side of the lake,' Mel repeated. He put the suitcase

25

down, and leaned on the glass counter. 'How far would that be, in miles?'

'Seven.'

'Uh huh. There wouldn't be a bus headed out there.'

'Nope.'

'I wonder how I get there.' The hangover was making him feel sickly humorous, like a condemned man noticing the hangman's fly is open.

'Beats me,' said the little man. 'You an actor?'

'It says here.'

'What's that?'

'It says I'm an actor.'

'The rest all came in yesterday. They sent the station wagon down. You could maybe phone.' He motioned at the phone booths in the back of the store.

'I bet that would work. Many thanks.'

He picked up the suitcase and carried it back by the booths, and put it down again. Hanging from a piece of string nailed to the wall was the phone book, a small slender staple-bound volume with a blue cover. After a lifetime spent looking up numbers in the Manhattan directory, this little blue book seemed unreal. Visions of Ray Bradbury danced in his head.

He found the theatre number, stepped into the booth, and made the call. A young-sounding female voice answered, and when he told her who and where he was she said, 'Oh. We were wondering about you. Just a minute.'

'What's a minute, at this stage?'

'That's right,' she said, and went away.

He waited, perspiring gently in the phone booth, shakes and headache both worse again now because he was standing up and no longer had the protection of the air-conditioned bus. He wanted a cigarette but he was afraid to light one, knowing what it would taste like.

The same voice came back after a while and told him to wait at the depot, someone would be down to get him. He thanked her and left the booth and went over to the lunch counter.

The little man in the white coat came over and asked him

what he wanted. He asked for coffee, and then changed his mind and asked for iced coffee. The little man said, 'No iced coffee. Iced tea.'

He was going to go into a Hemingway routine from that – repeat everything the little man said, and ask when the Swede came in for dinner – but he didn't have the energy. And the little man wouldn't get it, he'd figure Mel for a smart aleck. So he said, 'All right, iced tea.'

The iced tea helped, more than he'd expected, and he tried some Nabs, little sandwiches of crackers and peanut butter. After a while he even took a chance on a cigarette, and it tasted no worse than usual. About like the one before breakfast.

Twenty minutes after the phone call, a girl in a white shirt and jeans and sneakers came in and said, 'Mel Daniels?'

'More or less.'

'Come on along.'

He picked up his suitcase and followed her out to all that sunlight. A pale blue Ford station wagon shimmered in the No Parking zone. They got in and she drove, westward, toward the lake. The other traffic was mostly expensive cars, Cadillacs or Rolls or Continentals, Simonized to black glory.

'Mary Ann McKendrick,' said the girl abruptly. 'That's me.'

'Greetings. You already know who I am.'

'Indeed I do. Mr Haldemann is furious.'

'I had a going-away party. I kept going away, and going away, and going away.' He put his hands over his eyes. 'I should have brought sunglasses.'

'See if there's a pair in the glove compartment.'

He rummaged in the glove compartment and found a set of clip-ons. He balanced them on his nose and said, 'An inspector calls.'

She smiled, and said, 'Have you got an excuse worked out?'

'Not really.'

'Good. Your best bet is just to tell him the truth.'

'Dear Mr Haldemann. He was young once himself.'

'He still is.' She said it with an odd defensiveness.

He tried to look at her searchingly, but the clip-ons fell off.

Did she have her cap set for Herr Haldemann? He couldn't be sure.

Ah, well, there'd be other girls.

They were away from town now, but he couldn't see any lake. It should be off to the right, but the road on that side was lined with tall fencing, broken now and again by iron gates at the entrance to private roads. Through the fencing he could see parklike expanses of lawn and trees. Estates along here, to go with the rich cars.

On the other side of the road, the country was wilder and scrubbier, sloping steeply upward from the road, blending into the mountains that ringed town and lake.

He closed his eyes. His instinct was to talk with her – she was female, and pleasant to look at – but he just didn't have the strength. Faintly, he said, 'Remind me to talk to you tomorrow.'

'All right.' From the sound of her voice she was smiling again.

'I'll tell you the story of my life.'

'That'll be nice.'

They rode the rest of the way in silence, Mary Ann McKendrick driving and Mel recuperating. The world was orange on his closed eyelids; down inside there, he was untying his nerves.

He opened his eyes when the smoothness of blacktop under the Ford's tyres gave way to the chattering harshness of gravel. Ahead of him was a red barn, but redder than any barn he'd ever seen before, redder than Chinese red or fire-engine red, a bright bright red that made the barn look as though it were made of gleaming metal. Combined with the red were streaks and slashes of white trim, and great white block letters along the front that read:

CARTIER ISLE
THEATRE

The blue-grey gravel covered the entire expanse of ground between road and barn, and extended an additional pseudopod around to the right, between barn and house. The house – which he saw only after his eyes and brain got a little used to all that red barn – was a decrepit farmhouse, three storeys high, bulging with bay windows. There had apparently been no paint left over, because the clapboard siding of the house was weathered grey, the colour of driftwood.

Three cars were parked in front of the barn; a red MG – looking anaemic in these surroundings – an old black dusty Dodge coupé, and a white Continental convertible. Mary Ann McKendrick stopped the station wagon next to the other three, and said, 'Leave your bag here. You'd better go straight in and see Mr Haldemann.'

'Whatever you say.' He put the clip-ons back in the glove compartment. 'Is that where I live?' He pointed at the house.

'Uh huh.'

'I better buy a cross.'

She was properly baffled, like a good straight-woman. 'What? Why?'

'I'll tell you,' he said. 'A vampire comes in, and you wave a Star of David at him, he laughs in your face.'

'Oh. I wouldn't know about that.'

Was there a sudden chill in the air? Or was he just being oversensitive again? And why, he asked himself, did he always make a point of letting people know he was Jewish the minute he met them?

It was the wrong time for introspection; it just made his head ache more. Besides, Herr Haldemann was waiting.

He got out of the car. 'Where do I find the young Mr Haldemann?'

'Just inside. The office is to the right.'

'See you later.' But he had the feeling she didn't like him.

He walked across the gravel to the entrance, which had been lifted entire from some defunct movie house and spliced into the front of this structure, looking odd and anachronistic and somehow tilted out of true. Eight glass doors across in a row, reflecting Mel as he came walking up.

Inside, the lobby was very shallow and functional, with a red carpet, and a ticket window on the right. There were only two doors from lobby to theatre, at opposite ends of the lobby's rear wall. The wall between was covered with a montage of black-and-white photographs of actors and actresses and scenes from plays. Posters on the left-hand wall proclaimed the season's schedule and the names of the resident company, ten in all, six men and four women. Mel's name was third from the bottom, with only two girls' names beneath.

There was a juicy round blonde behind the ticket window, smiling at him in grateful appreciation of the difference between girls and boys. He went over and said, 'I'm looking for the office. I'm Mel Daniels.'

'Oh, you're the naughty boy.'

'You ain't seen nuthin' yet. Where's the office?'

'Through the door and to the right. I'm Cissie Walker.'

'You don't look sissy to me.'

She giggled, and tried without success to look demure.

So the hell with Mary Ann McKendrick.

He went through the door and to the right, and saw a door with the word *Office* on it. 'This must be the place,' he muttered, for his own amusement, and went on in.

It wasn't a small room, but it was so crowded with furniture it looked tiny. There were three large tables and two large desks, an assortment of chairs, and filing cabinets and wastebaskets and coatracks filling the space left over. Papers and posters littered every surface.

A man of about thirty-five, prematurely balding, very tall and lean, harried-looking, dressed in blue polo shirt and grey slacks, a yellow pencil behind one ear, sat at a desk and talked desperately on the telephone. He was the only one in the office. He said, 'But I *need* that sofa. We *paid* for that ottoman, Mr Gregory. . . . I understand that, Mr Gregory, but . . . '

It went on that way. Mel cleared a stack of programmes off a chair, put them on a table, and sat down. The man on the phone didn't acknowledge his presence at all. Mel waited a few minutes, listening to half the conversation and trying to guess at the other half, and then lit a cigarette. Immediately the man on the phone shoved an ashtray toward him. He nodded his thanks, and settled back to wait.

Finally it ended. They weren't going to get the sofa. The man hung up, looked at Mel, shook his head, and said, 'It's the same thing every year. You're Daniels, I guess.'

'That's right.'

'Actors are idiots, Daniels.' He didn't sound angry or sarcastic, only long-suffering. 'I don't know why I have anything to do with them. One sends me his room-mate's picture by mistake, one shows up a day late – I just don't know.'

'I guess you're Mr Haldemann.'

'I guess I am. I'm not sure any more. Mary Ann get you settled?'

'She told me to come in here first.'

'Oh. Well – ' He scrabbled through the mess on his desk. 'As long as you're here – ' He opened desk drawers. 'There's some forms to fill out. Withholding, and – ' He kept opening drawers. 'I don't suppose you have a pen.'

'They won't let me have anything sharp.'

'Uh? Oh. Actors are idiots? Nothing personal, Mel. Mel?'

'Mel.'

'That's right. Bob. I mean me, I'm Bob.'

'Hello.'

'Mm. Here we go. Just clear off a space on that table there. This won't take long.'

There was a form for the theatre's records, and a form for Equity, and the withholding form for taxes. He did the withholding form last and looked over at Bob Haldemann to say, 'On this tax form. Stage name or real name?'

'What? Legal name.'

'That's what I was afraid of.'

He wrote it out carefully: Melvin D. Blum. Which brought back to mind his argument with his father over the name-change. 'Dad, listen. Can you see it? In great big lights on Broadway, that brand-new star, Mel Blum. Forget it.' 'And what about Shelley Berman?' 'Berman is Berman, Blum is Blum.' 'A son of mine, to be ashamed of his heritage, is – ' 'What ashamed? Listen, do you know what Cary Grant's real name is?' 'Cary Grant is Jewish?' 'No, he's English. And his name is Archie Leach. You see what I mean? It isn't heritage, it's you got to have a good-looking name. You think anybody's *really* named Rock Hudson?' 'How am I supposed to hold my head up, I produced a son to change his name?' 'It's a *stage* name, for Christ's sake. *Every*body does it.' 'Shelley Berman – '

It got so you could hate Shelley Berman.

He finished the last of the forms, and brought them over to Bob Haldemann, who was laboriously writing on yellow note-paper with a stubby pencil. He took the forms and the pen and said, 'Sit down a minute, Mel.'

Mel sat down.

Bob Haldemann held the stubby pencil in both hands and, watching the pencil, said, 'This is your first season of stock, am I right?'

'Right.'

'Your experience – ' He riffled through the papers on his desk again. 'I don't have your résumé here. But you've been in a few off-Broadway shows, isn't that it?'

'That's it.'

'No other experience?'

'I toured with an Army show, I was in Special Services.'

'Oh?' He seemed surprised. 'How old are you?'

'Twenty-one.'

'No college?'

'I'm going to CCNY, part time.'

'Ah. And you're serious about acting.'

'Sure.' He said it easily, but who knew? He didn't know yet what he was serious about, but why rush it? He liked acting, and it put him close to girls, and if he could make a living at it, why not?

Bob Haldemann was still studying that pencil. He said, 'If you're at all like most of the young actors we get here, you aren't particularly interested in this theatre or this season. You're here for two things, a good time with the girls and an Equity card at the end of the season.'

That about summed it up, but it would probably be bad politics to admit it. Mel sat silent, and waited.

'I don't blame you, Mel. At your age, in your position, I'd feel the same way. But I want you to get interested in this theatre, and I want you to get interested in this season. I want total commitment from you, Mel, for the next eleven weeks. We have an impossibly tough schedule here, a new play every week. You'll have a major role in only four or five of them, but you'll be *working* in all of them. You'll be a stagehand, or you'll run the flies, or you'll work props. You'll help build sets, and you'll help strike them. You'll work a seven-day week, and you'll work a fourteen-hour day most of the time. You can't do that and last the season if you don't give a damn about what's happening here.'

Mel grinned. 'I guess I can't be doing it for the money.'

Bob Haldemann smiled back. 'I know. Thirty-five dollars a week can't buy the kind of work we'll need from you. Not even an Equity card can make it all worth it. The only thing that will keep you going is a commitment to this season and this theatre.' He broke off suddenly, and sat back in the chair, tossing the pencil down on his desk. 'I wish youd 'come in yesterday,' he said. 'This speech makes more sense when it's given to a whole group.'

'I know what you're saying, though,' Mel told him.

'Good. Do you think you can do the job?'

'You mean, on account of me coming in late?'

He shook his head and waved his hands, as though embarrassed. 'No, no, not at all. That's in the past. It was simply a rhetorical question, part of the speech. Believe me, Mel, I'm not trying to talk you into going back home. It's just part of the speech. If anybody ever took me up on it and said, "No, I don't think I can do the job, you better get another boy." I don't know what I'd do. You think I could get somebody to take your place this late in the season? New York is empty by now.'

'Oh.'

Haldemann got abruptly to his feet. 'Come on, I'll introduce you around, and then you can get settled in your room.'

'Okay. Thanks.'

Haldemann led the way out of the office. The theatre was in semi-darkness, lit only by work-lights from the stage. Somewhere, a power saw was whirring. The stage was empty, all the way back to the wooden rear wall, where some chairs were clustered.

They walked down the centre aisle and up the side steps to the stage. A young man in T-shirt and dungarees had disembowelled the light-board and was standing looking at the wreckage, holding a screwdriver. Haldeman introduced him as Perry Kent, and Kent nodded distractedly. 'Perry's run the lights for us for the last three years,' said Haldemann. 'Come on this way.'

They crossed the stage to the other side, toward the sound of the power saw. The stage was large – thirty-some feet wide, and almost as deep – with large wings. The light-board was to stage right, with the fly loft above. To stage left, the wing was stacked high with platforms and flats and odd sticks of furniture. High above, the flown drops swayed very slowly.

Haldemann went first, threading his way through the junk stacked up to the left of the stage, and over to a door on the side wall. He opened it, and the sound of the saw was suddenly much louder. It shut off as Mel came through the doorway.

It was a small room, with an incredibly high ceiling. Two dusty windows high up on the side wall let in practically no sun; light came from a bare bulb suspended from a crossbeam. Flats were stacked against all the walls, in a jumble of old sets, a twelve-foot pale green flat next to an eighteen-foot maroon flat with a false window overlooking mountain scenery, a white door-flat with a blue door next to a narrow ten-footer splashed with all the colours of the rainbow. Long lengths of pine jutted up above it all from one corner.

In a cleared space in the middle was a scarred worktable, and on the table the power handsaw. Next to the table stood a tall fat man with steel-rimmed spectacles, wearing a blue T-shirt and dirty white bib overalls. Haldemann introduced him as Arnie Kapow, carpenter / designer.

Kapow shook Mel's hand, his grip surprisingly soft for such a big man. He said. 'You know anything about flat sizes?'

'Some.'

'You come work with me when you get settled. All right, Bob?'

'If it's all right with Ralph.'

'Up Ralph.' Kapow turned away and switched the saw on again. The buzzing made any more conversation impossible.

Haldemann motioned to Mel, and they went back out to the stage area. 'Arnie's not much of a talker,' Haldemann said, apologizing, 'but wait'll you see his work.'

Mel shrugged. This whole tour was a waste of time anyway. You met people by working with them, not by walking in and out of rooms. Haldemann was wasting time on him this way because he was late; Haldemann was bending over backward to show Mel it was all right.

There was a wide double door at the rear of the stage. Haldemann opened it, and they went out to the sunlight. This double door was a loading entrance, with a three-foot jump to the ground. They jumped, and walked to the left, where two girls were hosing flats, and scrubbing them with GI brushes. Haldemann explained. 'We don't have any permanent sets, so we use water-soluble paint. Kemtone. Wash it off and you can use the flat all over again.'

'Why not just paint over it?'

'Weight. You'd be surprised how much five or six coats of paint can weigh.'

Haldemann introduced him to the girls, but he didn't get their full names. Linda was the childish-looking redhead, and Karen was the emaciated brunette. Both were sopping, and soap-covered, and desperate-looking. They stood dripping, and acknowledged the introductions with hysterical smiles. If he remembered right, they were the ones whose names appeared under his on the poster in the lobby.

From there, they went around to the front of the theatre, Haldemann saying, 'The rest are over at the house. You might as well pick up your bag on the way.'

'Okay.'

'Don't mind Ralph, when you see him,' Haldemann cautioned gently. 'He isn't the most tactful person in the world. But he's a really first-rate director. You can learn a lot from him.'

The station wagon was still out front, with the other three cars. Heldemann frowned at the dusty Dodge and said, to himself, 'Mary Ann still here?' To Mel he said, 'I'll be with you in just a second.'

Mel got his suitcase and walked over to the entrance, where Haldemann was standing with one of the glass doors held open, his head tilted inside. Looking past him, Mel saw Mary Ann McKendrick behind the ticket window now, instead of the pneumatic Cissie. Mary Ann was apparently saying something, though Mel was too far away to hear it. He heard Haldemann answer, 'All right. I'll see you tomorrow.' Then he turned, saw Mel, and said, 'All right. You've got your bag? Yes, I see. Good.'

They walked together across the gravel toward the house. Mel said, 'Mary Ann's a local girl?'

'Yes. I thought she'd be gone by now, but she's taken over for Cissie for a few minutes.'

They went up the sagging stoop and into the house. A dim hall stretched ahead of them, and voices came through the closed doors to their right. Haldemann opened these doors – double doors, that slid back into the wall – and stuck his head in, saying, 'Excuse me, Ralph. Daniels is here.' He sounded apologetic again, as though this Ralph were the employer and Haldemann only a very minor flunky.

'How nice.' It was a coarse gravelly voice, heavy with sarcasm. 'Shall we give him a drum roll?'

Mel set his suitcase down in the hall, and followed Haldemann through the doorway.

It was a long room, made by the removal of the partition between living and dining-rooms, used now as a rehearsal hall. Folding chairs were scattered around in no particular order on the bare floor, and at the far end of the room there was a cleared space containing only a beat-up sofa and an old kitchen table.

Four men were sitting here and there on the folding chairs. A man and a woman stood up by the sofa, holding playbooks open in their hands. Another man stood in a corner at the back of the room, a cigar in his mouth.

Haldemann said, 'Ralph Schoen, Mel Daniels.'

Ralph Schoen was the man with the cigar. He was of medium height, and very fat. The second fat man Mel had met so far today. But Arnie Kapow was fat in a solid, hard sort of way; he was barrel-shaped. And Ralph Schoen was shaped like a bag of lard, soft and sagging, with a petulant jowly face, and pudgy hands. He was wearing a grey suit and white shirt and bright red tie, the tie pulled loose from his throat and the shirt bunched at his waist where the coat hung open.

He came forward, removing the cigar from his mouth. 'You're Daniels, huh?'

The man was offensive just by his very nature. The look of him was offensive, and the sound of his voice was offensive. Added to it, he was at the moment *trying* to be offensive.

More than anything else in the world, Mel wanted to hit him in the mouth. But he just said, 'That's right. I'm Daniels.'

'Isn't that wonderful. What's your experience, Daniels?'

'What?'

'Experience, experience. You have *some* experience, haven't you?'

'Four off-Broadway shows, if that's what you mean.'

'How many lines?'

'Lines?'

Schoen grimaced. 'That's what I like,' he said. 'Quick on the uptake. I'll go a little slower for you, Daniels.' He held up one pudgy hand, extended one finger, waved it. 'The first show you were in, Daniels. How many lines did you have?'

'Two.'

Another finger. 'Second show.'

'None. I was in three crowd scenes.'

'Crowd scenes! Off-Broadway is getting expensive!' Another finger. 'Third show.'

'Five lines.'

'And fourth show.'

'Three lines.'

'And that's it? No more experience? *Professional* experience, I mean, Daniels. I'm not interested in your high-school play.'

'That's it. Just the four shows.'

'Do you even have an Equity card, Daniels?'

'No.'

'Then tell me, Daniels.' Schoen smirked at him, and stuck the cigar back in his mouth, and talked around the cigar. 'Just tell me, Daniels, do you really think you're ready for the grand entrance yet?'

'I'm not trying to make any grand en –'

'Or am I misjudging you? Do you just happen to come from a part of the world where the calendar is different? Do you live the other side of the International Date Line, Daniels?'

Mel opened his mouth to call Schoen a fat slob, just to relieve his feelings, but Haldemann cut in first, saying, 'He's here now, Ralph. I think we can let bygones be bygones.'

'Of course.' Schoen smiled around his cigar and shook his head. 'I can hardly wait for your first entrance, Daniels,' he said. 'The cue is delivered, there's a pregnant pause, everyone on stage looks toward the door where you should be coming in, and where are you?'

'Still here listening to you, I guess.'

Haldemann spoke hurriedly again, burying about half of Mel's line: 'Arnie says he can use Mel today if you don't need him, Ralph.'

'Need him? *Need* him? Perish the thought. No, we went ahead and cast our first production without you, Daniels. A real shame. I'm looking forward to seeing you act.'

Haldemann touched Mel's arm. 'Come along,' he said, rather hurriedly. 'You can meet the others later.'

Mel followed him out to the hall. Haldemann closed the double doors and said, 'His bark is worse than his bite, Mel, it really is. If you're afraid he'll be down on you all season, don't worry. He'll forget all about this by tomorrow.'

'Great.'

'We're all under pressure here, Mel. Don't let Ralph get under your skin.'

'Perish the thought.'

Haldemann smiled, nervously. 'You go on up and find yourself a room now,' he said. 'Get changed into work clothes, and then report to Arnie.'

'Right.'

'Just try doors up there. We all keep our room doors locked. You never know who'll come into the house here.'

Which meant, Mel knew, there'd been a history of petty thieving here. And it would be some member of the company doing it, no stranger wandering in from outside.

He was beginning to wonder if summer stock was such a good idea.

Haldemann went out, with one last encouraging smile, and Mel took his suitcase and went upstairs. There were six doors in the second-floor hall, and five of them were locked. The sixth was the bathroom. So he went on up to the third floor.

Another six doors. The first two were locked, but the third one opened. Mel stepped inside, looked around, and froze.

Cissie Walker was lying on the bed. She was wearing white socks and one sleeve of her blouse. The rest of her clothing, ripped to pieces, was scattered around the room. Her arms and legs were spread-eagled, and her fingers were curved into taut claws. Red streaked her face, and the pillow beneath her head. Her throat was livid with grey and purple bruises. Her tongue protruded, fat and dry, from her crushed mouth. Her eyes were red and staring, straining up out of her face like gory marbles. A band of yellow sunlight angled across her chest.

Mel turned, stumbling, and took two steps, and vomited in the hall.

The madman had forgotten about women.

He'd forgotten the feel of their thighs, the roundness of their rumps, the heavy promise of their breasts. He'd forgotten the clothes they wore, and they way they walked, and the way their arms moved, and the lines of their throats, and the softness of their lips, and the looks in their eyes. He'd forgotten the sound of their voices, and the way they smiled, and the way they climbed stairs or sat in a chair or bent over a table.

He'd forgotten about women; so he forgot to be clever.

The awareness hadn't really started until he'd gotten to the theatre. There had been women on the bus, and women on the streets of Cartier Isle, but then he'd been too full of his plans, thinking and scheming and trying to find fault with the way he'd worked it all out. It wasn't until he was set, until Haldemann had accepted the idiotic story of the wrong photograph, until the madman was sure no one suspected him, that the awareness had really started.

It had begun with Mary Ann McKendrick. She had a good-looking face, but that was secondary. It was the body that drew him. She wore tight blue jeans, and he could almost feel the rough texture beneath his palm, him stroking her legs. His palms grew damp and he kept staring at her, watching the movement of her, imagining her without the blue jeans, imagining himself conjoined with her. He tried to visualize her breasts, too, but the man's white shirt she wore was too loose for accurate observation.

He watched her all during Haldemann's opening speech, in the theatre on Wednesday afternoon. Haldemann and Ralph Schoen stood up on the stage, and the company sat in the first few rows below them. There were five actors and four actresses, the light man, the stage manager, the carpenter, and Mary Ann McKendrick. Mary Ann McKendrick wasn't an actress. She was Haldemann's secretary, and she did the theatre's publicity, and she would be assistant director throughout the season and hold the prompt book during rehearsals.

Mary Ann moved around a lot during that first meeting, Wednesday afternoon. She distributed the forms for all of them to fill out, and ball-point pens to those who didn't have pens of their own. And during the speechmaking she sat on the stage apron, up where the madman could stare at her.

Haldemann talked about how much work they would do this summer, and how they would have to give the theatre total commitment if they expected to last the season, and all through his speech the madman stared at Mary Ann McKendrick. Then Ralph Schoen made a speech, telling them that summer stock too often meant theatre one notch below amateur, but that in *his* summer stock theatre they were going to be professionals. From what he said, the three leads – Loueen Campbell and Richard Lane and Alden March – had all been here for other seasons and were local favourites. Ralph Schoen expected the new people to give Loueen and Dick and Alden good professional support. He would accept no less.

While Schoen grated on, the madman watched Mary Ann. He felt safe now, and comfortable. He had a place to sleep, and a way to get food, and he would be getting money every week. He had a safe refuge, complete with credentials. He had been accepted. He could relax now, and stare at Mary Ann McKendrick, and remember about women.

It hadn't been anything to do with women, his having been sent to the asylum. He had killed two people, but they had both been men, co-workers of his.

But the four years in the asylum had changed him. The restaints of civilization had held him tenuously at best; in civilization's attacking him with Doctor Chax and his shock therapy, with the isolation ward and the hard-handed male nurses, civilization had lost him completely.

He knew of no reason why he shouldn't take anything he wanted.

When the speechmaking was finished, they all went over next door to have a late lunch. A woman named Mrs Kenyon had made the lunch. She was a local woman who came every day of the season to cook the meals and clean the house. They all sat at the long table in the room beside the kitchen, and Mrs Kenyon served them lunch.

All but Mary Ann McKendrick. She was local, too, and didn't eat with the rest of the company. So the madman looked around the table, the hunger sharpening in him with the departure of its first object.

There were four women at the table. Loueen Campbell, the female lead of the company, was in her middle thirties, a hard-looking woman with most of the femininity beaten out of her. He looked at her, and looked away. Not her.

Linda Murchieson had bright red hair, but she looked like a child. She had a child's vacuous face, and childishly thin arms, and childishly small breasts. There was a kind of innocent sexuality to her, but it was too subtle an appeal to reach him now. Maybe later, when the first raw ache of the hunger had been satisfied.

Karen Leacock failed for much the same reason. She looked to be in her early twenties, but she was even thinner than Linda

Murchieson, with a thin face; thin-lipped thin-nosed, bony.

His eyes were drawn to Cissie Walker.

Roundness. All roundness, but not fat. Not at all fat. Just roundnesses and roundnesses. She would be soft to the touch, soft and yielding. She would enfold him in musk and warmth and softness. Anywhere he reached, he would find a roundness to fit his cupped hand.

She saw him staring at her, and she blushed, and giggled, and dropped her eyes. And then she looked at him sidelong, and smiled.

In this house there were fourteen beds. Two on this floor, where Haldemann and Schoen had their rooms. Six on the second floor, six on the third floor. All the women had rooms to themselves, and most of the actors had rooms to themselves. Arnie Kapow, the carpenter, shared a room on the second floor with the light man, Perry Kent. And Tom Burns, the stage manager, shared a third-floor room with Alden March, one of the two male leads.

Fourteen beds. Ten rooms that contained only one bed each.

Ten rooms where he could take Cissie Walker, and ease the hunger. Four years; ten rooms; fourteen beds. The numbers circled in his mind, circling images of himself and Cissie Walker.

After lunch, he would get her away from the rest, take her to one of the ten rooms.

But after lunch there was no time. After lunch they all went to work.

Ralph Schoen cast the first play then and there, over the empty lunch dishes. The play was titled *The Merry Widow of Vichy*, and was a tragicomedy about the wartime years in Vichy, France, during the Pétain republic. Loueen Campbell was the widow of the title, the widow of a French general who had died in the first German advance. Richard Lane and Alden March were the two politicians vying for her favour. There were only these three major parts, plus five minor roles. So only two of the ten members of the company would not have parts in the first play. The actor who hadn't shown up yet was one, and

Cissie Walker was the other. She would work in the box office, and would also take care of props.

She went away to the box office right after lunch. And the madman had to stay with the rest, had to go into the rehearsal room with them and go through a reading of the play. And then the male members of the cast were taken away by Arnie Kapow to work in the theatre. They spent the next seven hours lowering backdrops from the flies, looking at them, taking them down and rolling them and putting them away at the back of the stage, moving them back and forth from one spot in the flies to another, bringing more up from the storage space under the stage. The madman and Perry Kent worked up in the fly loft, raising and lowering the drops, tying them off and reweighting the carriages. It was hot cramped work, heavy work, and the madman lost himself in the labour. For those hours up in the fly loft he was almost happy; a free human being, working his body as it was meant to be worked, stretching his muscles, straining at the ropes, and working in silent comradeship with other men. At the infrequent breaks, when he and Perry climbed down to the stage to sit with the others and smoke a cigarette, he was at peace. He forgot to be wary, forgot to be afraid. They talked together, and laughed together, and he joined with them and felt himself a part of them.

This was his true self. Not that beast forced to murder an old man and an old woman. How he'd hated that! How he hated the world that had made it necessary.

If only the whole world could be like this. Men working together in harmony, without suspicion, without fear. Without cruelty.

He hoped he would never be forced to kill any of these men. He hoped it with all his heart.

It was one in the morning when they finally stopped work, and they all trooped back to the house for a late snack in the kitchen before going to bed. The madman felt a delicious exhaustion, a comfortable drowsiness. The kitchen was bright and warm; the faces around him were happy and tired.

How *good* this was! He nearly wept at the beauty of it.

He was so tired, when at last they all went upstairs to their beds, that he didn't even think of Cissie Walker. He just went into his room and undressed and crawled between clean sheets and fell immediately asleep.

Thursday morning, the mood of the night before was still with him. He revelled in the comradeship of the breakfast table, the automatic way in which the others accepted him as one of them. He glanced at Cissie Walker and was pleased by her, but only as a pleasant member of this pleasant company. The hunger of yesterday afternoon had disappeared completely.

It came back slowly during the day. In the morning, the men worked with Arnie Kapow, carrying flats out back for the girls to wash. For now, they were only concerned with the flats for the first week's set. They carried out the flats Arnie selected, and then they went back to the stage to lay the ground-cloth and to fly the cyclorama. While the work was being done on the cyc, the madman was up in the fly loft with Perry again. Looking down through the ropes at the stage, he saw Mary Ann McKendrick moving around down there, checking the furniture list with Arnie. And Cissie Walker brought them coffee twice. She was the only girl in blouse and skirt; the others all wore blue jeans. Looking down at the stage from the fly loft, the madman watched Mary Ann McKendrick and Cissie Walker, and the hunger began again, building slowly.

And it built more after lunch. Ralph Schoen started the first rehearsal then. He didn't need Linda and Karen, so they went back to work for Arnie some more, but he did need all the men.

Ralph gave them copies of the play, the acting version published by Samuel French. Then, while the rest of them just sat around, Ralph concentrated on the opening scene between Loueen Campbell and Richard Lane.

Loueen Campbell was playing the merry widow, a sophisticated nymphomaniac with a gift for smug repartee. Even in this first rehearsal, reading from the playbook, she was working at getting the character across. She was wearing a white blouse and black slacks, and her body was solid-looking, heavily girdled. Her hard and somewhat bitter face suited the character she was playing, adding just the slightest touch of coarseness to the widow's sensuality.

The madman watched. He stared at her, and the imaginings began to build up again, with this time yet another leading lady, and he fabricated ways to get her alone. His mind invented entire sequences of lust with Loueen Campbell, in all of which she was, if anything, even more eager than he.

Late in the afternoon he had to answer a call of nature which was distracting him from his daydreams. There was no bathroom on the first floor, so he went upstairs, and on the way back down he met Cissie Walker coming up.

'Hi, there,' she said. She smiled. 'How's it going with mean ol' Ralph?'

He stared at her, unable for a second to say anything at all. But he had to say *something*, before the silence became unnatural. 'It's all right,' he muttered finally, and grimaced at the flatness of it.

She went on by, smiling, and as she passed him she gave him another of those sidelong looks from the corner of her eye. He stopped, six steps from the bottom, but could think of nothing to say.

It wasn't his kind of cleverness. He had learned to be clever, but only in a certain way, only in the direction of silence and deception. The kind of cleverness that found things to say to women was something else entirely.

He turned and looked up after her. Her rump switched back and forth as she went up the stairs, making the skirt flare this way and that. She was wearing loafers and white socks; her legs were bare. Looking up, he saw her bare legs halfway up the thighs, in brief glimpses through the swaying skirt. Pale shadowed thighs, hidden away within the skirt.

She was the one. Not Loueen Campbell or Mary Ann McKendrick or anyone else at all. Cissie Walker was the one.

Because she had such a round body. And because she looked at him sidelong out of the corner of her eye. And because she *would* be eager, he was sure of it. As eager as he himself. As eager as Loueen Campbell in his daydreams.

He heard her go on up the stairs to the third floor, and after a minute he followed her.

Cleverness. Cleverness. He had to know what he was going to say before he got there. He had to be ready to say witty things, funny things, but suggestive things.

Like the people in *The Merry Widow of Vichy*. They were always saying witty and suggestive things to one another, and smiling.

His own face was frozen; he looked sullen and bitter and enraged, and defiantly afraid. He stopped in the second-floor hallway to try to make his face more pleasant. He stretched his lips wide in a grimace, hoping they would fall into a smile. He pressed his cheeks with the palms of his hands, and his cheeks were cold.

Was this any way? He had to appeal to her, he had to make her want him. He couldn't be silent and frozen-faced.

But he could think of nothing witty to say to her. And he couldn't make the muscles of his face relax. His hands clenched into fists, and he beat his fists together, furious at himself.

He had to *think*. He would go upstairs, up to her room. She would look up and see him. What would she say?

She would ask him what he was doing there.

He would say . . .

'Life is too boring downstairs.'

He whispered it aloud. 'Life is too boring downstairs.' And – 'I have better things to do.'

And she would say: 'Oh? What things?'

He would glance meaningfully at her breasts. 'All sorts of things.'

What would she say then?

He couldn't think. He had no idea what she would say then.

But at least he had a beginning, he had something to get the conversation going. Once they were talking together, he would think of more things to say. The important part was to get started.

He went on upstairs to the third floor.

All the doors but one were closed. He went over to the open doorway and looked in. She was sitting on the bed. She was taking off her right shoe; her right leg was crossed over the left, hiking her skirt up to her hips. A band of yellow sunlight gleamed on her bare legs.

She saw him standing there, and leaped to her feet, pushing her skirt down over her legs. She was very angry. She snapped, 'What the hell are you, a Peeping Tom?'

It was the wrong beginning, but he tried to keep to his part of the script. He smiled at her, a shaky and nervous smile, and said, 'Life is too boring downstairs.' The words came out flat, like the memorized speech they were.

'Listen, you get away from here,' she said. 'You want me to tell Bob Haldemann?'

He stepped into the room, his hands out in front of him in a pleading gesture. 'I just want to be friends,' he said.

'You pick a funny way to be friends.' She flounced over to the closet, with only white socks on her feet, and got another pair of shoes, a pair of white sneakers. They reminded him of the asylum, and Doctor Chax.

He couldn't help himself any more. He crossed the room and reached out and touched her arms, the flesh warm beneath his fingers. 'Cissie – ' he said.

'Now *listen*.'

She was backing up, more angry than frightened, and he kept moving toward her. She tried to push his hands away, and he gripped her arms, refusing to let go. 'Be a good girl, Cissie,' he said, his voice a harsh whisper. 'Be a good girl.'

'Get *away* from me. You crazy nut, you want me to scream?'

Scream. People coming. Shouts. Suspicion. Questions. Exposure. Doctor Chax.

She couldn't be allowed to scream.

He moved his right hand back and formed it into a fist and drove it at her face.

Her eyes widened, and then she was falling backward, turning as she fell because his left hand still gripped her right arm. But she was still conscious, wide-eyed, her mouth red with lipstick and now red with blood and now opening wide to scream, and he hit her again. The force of it knocked her down, and the momentum knocked him down on top of her, and suddenly she was wriggling beneath him, her body hot and alive. She was squirming and struggling, trying to get free, but the movements of her tore him apart, the hunger was a physical pain, an absolute necessity.

She had to stop fighting him. She had to give in and let him feed the hunger. She had to stop trying to get away.

His hands found her throat. They tightened.

Her right ear was near his mouth, and his nostrils were full of the musk of her. He whispered, 'Don't fight me, Cissie, don't make me hurt you. I don't want to hurt you. I want us to have fun together, Cissie, don't make me hurt you. Stop fighting me, Cissie. Stop fighting me and I'll let go your throat.'

But she fought and fought, she squirmed and lunged, her legs beat at him, her arms flailed, her body lifted and twisted beneath him. If she'd had shoes on they would have made a drumming racket on the floor and, though they were on the third floor and the nearest other people were two flights down, still someone might have heard the noise and come to see what the drumming on the floor was all about. But her feet were shod only in white socks. No one heard.

He clung to her, his body pressing down on hers, his hands clenched tight on her throat. He pleaded with her not to fight him, he told her over and over that he didn't want to hurt her, he begged her to let him have what he wanted without this struggling.

And gradually, he saw, his arguments were getting through to her. Her flailing and fighting lessened and slackened, more and more, and he whispered to her more fiercely, telling her what he wanted of her, promising her pleasure, and finally she understood that he really didn't want to hurt her this way, and she stopped fighting and lay beneath him acquiescent.

He smiled, pleased. He moved slightly, so his right hand could stroke her body, and he whispered, 'I'm glad, Cissie. We can have good times. I've been very lonely, Cissie. But not here on the floor, that's no good. You'll hurt your back. On the bed, Cissie. No, don't move, I'll carry you to the bed. Like a bride, Cissie.'

She was dead. He knew she was dead, but he refused to know

it. She wasn't dead. He could hear her breathing in his ear, he could feel the pounding of her heart in her chest against his chest. She was only frightened, afraid to move.

He reassured her, whispering to her, telling her time and time again that he had no wish to harm her. He crawled off her and picked her up and set her down gently on the bed. 'Shall I undress you?' he asked her.

Her eyes were open, but she only stared at the ceiling. She wouldn't look at him.

Rage suddenly filled him. She wanted to cheat him. She wanted to scare him. She was playing dead. She didn't really want to go to bed with him at all.

'We'll see!' He yanked at her skirt, ripping it at the seam, tearing it off. 'You think you can fool me! We'll see about that!'

He tore her clothing off, ripping the blouse and skirt to pieces, so one sleeve of the blouse still remained behind on her arm. He hooked his fingers inside her bra and yanked, and material ripped. He tore her clothing off, till she wore only the white socks and the sleeve of the blouse. And then he fell upon her.

She wouldn't move. No matter what he did, no matter how he tried to excite her, she wouldn't move. She didn't want to give him the satisfaction. He rutted on her, cursing her and pleading with her, and she refused to move.

When it was over, he suddenly knew that she really was dead. She was dead. She'd been dead all the time, since before he picked her up from the floor.

He scrabbled away from her, falling off the bed, scrambling to his feet and backing away across the room. A superstitious fear had filled him, leaving him weak and trembling. He had defiled a corpse. Her ghost had stood at the foot of the bed and watched him all the time.

He stared around the room, seeing shapes and figures and darknesses that swam and blurred, that vanished before he could focus his eyes. He heard sighing, and whispered words that he could not quite make out.

He stumbled out of the room, and down the stairs to the

second floor, fleeing blindly, without plan or purpose. But in the second-floor hallway he forced himself to stop, to stand still until he could start to think again.

She was dead. The rest was unimportant, it didn't matter. What did it matter? She was dead now, but how did he know when she died? Hadn't he heard her breath, felt her heartbeat? She had died afterward. Or she had died during. Or so what if she had died before? He couldn't be sure when she'd died, and it didn't matter, it was unimportant.

She'd brought it on herself anyway.

Flaunting herself at him. Giving him the sidelong looks. Smiling in that suggestive way. Swinging her body in front of him.

She had *asked* for it. By first promising him release, and then by turning him away. How *vicious* that was! She'd deserved to die.

But what was he to do now? They would find her body, sooner or later. What was he to do?

He could run. He could run away again, as he had run away from the asylum.

But it was *unfair*. He was happy here. He was safe here, and content. He was with people he liked. It was unfair that he should have to give all this up, just because that stupid girl had forced him to kill her.

Could he stay?

He had an alibi. He was downstairs at the rehearsal. Yes, he'd left the room for a few minutes, but so had everybody else at one time or another. He would be suspect, but so would everyone else.

And they needn't even think it was a member of the company. The front door was unlocked. Anyone could have come in, anyone at all. A stranger, a prowler.

He couldn't take a chance on it. If it looked as though they might catch up with him, he would have to run away. Otherwise, he'd take a chance on it.

He hurried into the bathroom to wash his face and hands, to adjust his clothing and look at himself in the mirror to be sure he bore no signs of what had happened. There were no signs.

He was clean. He could go back downstairs. He could stay on here with these people.

He loved these people. They had taken him in, they were good to him.

And all at once he felt sad. Because they had all liked Cissie Walker. They would be unhappy that she was dead. They would miss her.

He was unhappy, too, about her death. Because it would make his new friends sad. And because she had only been a foolish girl, not a mean girl. What had happened had been no more her fault than his. She had just been very young and silly, and hadn't realized the effect she had on men. And he had been too long away from women, and hadn't realized she didn't really mean the promises she seemed to make.

Would this spoil things? It had been a mistake, that's all, they'd both been mistaken, and the result had been inevitable. He hadn't wanted to kill her, he hadn't gone up there to kill her. He had *intended* to kill that old man and old woman, but he hadn't intended to kill Cissie Walker.

He wanted them to understand that. Not Doctor Chax; he had no explanations for Doctor Chax. His new friends, they were the ones. He wanted them to know he hadn't meant it, he wished it hadn't happened. He couldn't tell them so without them knowing it was he who had killed her, but he wanted them to know.

There was a bar of soap on the sink. He picked it up and wrote with it on the mirror:

I'M SORRY

That was all. They would understand. After all, he didn't *have* to write that there, so they would know he meant it sincerely.

He put the soap back on the sink, wiped his hands again on the towel, and went back down to the rehearsal room. He'd been gone no more than ten minutes.

The scene was still going on. Everyone was watching Loueen and Dick. No one paid any attention to him when he came in and sat down.

Five minutes later, Ralph Schoen had them turn to another scene, in which all of them appeared. The madman carried his playbook up to the front of the room with the others, and went through the scene with them. It was a brief scene, and then Ralph talked to them, criticizing their interpretations of the characters, though most of them had simply read the lines with no attempt yet at characterization. And then they were interrupted by Bob Haldemann, bringing in the actor who was a day late. It was a short interruption, and when it ended, Ralph had them go through the group scene again.

They'd barely started reading when they heard the shouts begin. Shrill male cries: 'Help! Help!' And heavy footsteps thudding down the stairs.

Eric Sondgard had been back on the job barely three days when the call came from the summer theatre. Joyce Ravenfield – mayor's daughter, City Hall receptionist, one-woman clerical staff, answerer of calls to all city departments including the police force – this Joyce Ravenfield buzzed Eric Sondgard's office at precisely four thirty-six. 'Call from the theatre, Eric,' she said. 'They say there's been a murder.'

'Are they still on the line?' He hadn't reacted at all to the terrible word; later on, he'd have leisure to wonder about that. Another psychic tooth to poke at.

'Yes, I think so.'

'Tell them not to touch anything. Call Mike, have him get out there. Tell him just hold the fort, don't *do* anything.'

'Right.'

'Find Dave. He's probably at the boat. Tell him to come here and mind the store till I get back.'

'Will do. Should I wake the boy?'

She meant Larry Temple, who was working night patrol, and who wouldn't be waking up for another two or three hours.

Sondgard said, 'No, let him sleep. We won't be needing any extra manpower.'

'Okay. Anything else?'

'Yes. Get in touch with Captain Whitsisname at the trooper barracks. You know, down at the foot of Fourteen.'

'Captain Garrett.'

'That's it. I don't know why I can't remember that name. Captain Garrett. Tell him we've got a murder reported, and I'm on my way to check it out. If there's anything in it, I'll call him direct from the scene.'

'Why do you need Captain Garrett, Eric?'

'Come on, Joyce. We're traffic cops. Even if we had the training and the experience to handle criminal investigation, which we don't, we still don't have the necessary equipment. Was the dead man shot?'

'I don't know, and it –'

'Say he was. We don't have the equipment for a ballistics check. We can't run a simple paraffin test on suspects' hands. I don't think a one of us could get a clean fingerprint from a mirror.'

'We ask the state to handle the science for us, Eric. That's what the state's for. But we don't have to go running to Captain Garrett the minute the complaint comes in. You always down-grade yourself, Eric. You always –'

'Don't start analyzing me, Joyce, you'll just depress yourself. I'll call you from the theatre.'

'All right, Eric,' she said, with exaggerated resignation.

He hung up, got his officer's cap, and left the office. Downstairs there was a giant mirror on the side wall, the architect's futile attempt to make a tiny marble lobby look like a great big marble court. Sondgard saw himself in it, a thin man in a pale blue uniform complete with knee-high black boots. 'Cossack,' he whispered at the reflection, and felt a little better. Stupid uniform.

Mike had the prowl car, of course. Mike always had the prowl car. Joyce would find him out at the practice range, shooting guns. Sondgard went around to the parking lot at the side of the building and got into his little black Volvo. He drove out to Broad Avenue and turned left, toward the lake.

Captain Eric Sondgard, forty-one years old, a man of titles. In June and July and August he bore the title *Captain*, and ran Cartier Isle's four-man police force. From September till May he bore the title *Professor* – Associate Professor really – and taught the Humanities in a Connecticut college.

'There's a dichotomy in you, Captain Professor,' he told himself. 'Half of you is a humanist and half of you is a Cossack. You're all mixed up, Professor Captain.'

He was talking to himself. Out loud. As soon as he realized it, he gave a snort of disgust and turned on the car radio. There was no local radio station, and the distant stations picked up a heavy load of static on their beamed way up through the mountains, but at least there was noise in the car now, and a part of the noise was discernibly a human voice. He wasn't totally alone now, and he wouldn't be talking to himself out loud.

He hadn't always felt this way. But six years of marriage had ended, seven years ago, in an emotional and sloppy divorce, full of bitterness and recrimination, and one of the side effects of that breakdown had been this dislike for solitude, this watchful fear that he would turn into a mumbling recluse, divorced from the world as well as his wife.

This job, summer Cossack, was in its way another side effect of the divorce. He and Janice had always spent their summers together in the cottage on Stenner Lake, but Janice had received the cottage as part of the settlement. The first summer without her, he had spent his time in his apartment in the city, and being alone at the wrong time of the year in the apartment where he had lived so long with Janice had nearly driven him crazy. The second summer he had taken a camp counsellor's job, not because he needed the money but simply to have something to do and the reassurance of other people around him, and he had detested the job. That fall, through a student, he had heard of the vacancy in the Cartier Isle police force. The student's family owned one of the estates on Black Lake,

54

and through them Sondgard had obtained the job. And surprised himself by liking it. This was his fifth summer at Cartier Isle; he would probably spend every summer here for the rest of his life.

Cartier Isle was a strange town, really; at least in that part of the year when he saw it. In the off-season months it was a tiny quiet community of seventeen hundred, and Mike Tompkins served as its entire police force. But during the summer it was a resort town, with a population swollen to over five thousand, and with the police force increased to four – Sondgard himself, and Dave Rand, the Floridian who ran a boat for fishing parties off the Florida coast the rest of the year and operated the police launch on Black Lake during the summer, and a student of Sondgard's, a different one each year, hired by him at the end of the school term. This year it was Larry Temple.

The policing of Cartier Isle in the summertime was complicated by two factors: first, the artificial boundaries of the town; and second, the type of people who were its summer residents.

The summer residents were, to begin with, wealthy. Cartier Isle was no middle-class vacation spot. There were no cottages for rent anywhere around Black Lake, no tourist cabins, no boat-rental agencies. Black Lake had become fashionable as a summer resort in the early twenties, when the first of the big lake-front estates were built, and it had never lost either its popularity or its wealthy atmosphere. The lake was ringed by the estates, big country homes surrounded by parks and tamed woods, fronting on private beaches, enclosed by high fencing, protected by uniformed guards driving black Mercurys or Buicks.

And the whole thing was within Sondgard's jurisdiction. As a result of political manoeuvring in the twenties, the entire frontage all around the lake was included within the official Cartier Isle town boundaries. The early estate owners had urged the move, so the town could then zone the area to keep the rabble out, and the town fathers had approved the idea because they could then tax the estates. Because the town kept its tax

55

bite modest, and because the estate owners usually refrained from interfering with local affairs, the arrangement worked out to the satisfaction of both sides.

But it still made life more complicated for Captain Eric Sondgard. This killing, now, out at the summer theatre. If the town had a sensible perimeter, the killing would have taken place seven miles outside town, and would have been either a county or state affair. State most likely, since the county organization was a petrified political fossil, with a sheriff who lived thirty miles away down the mountain in Monetta, and who hadn't left the town of Monetta in thirty years.

Even without this killing, there were complications enough. Circle South and Circle North, being the two halves of the road around the lake, had to be patrolled by the town police. The one or two drownings in the lake every summer were a town affair, though state dredging equipment was used to search for the bodies. Every bus into town was met either by Mike Tompkins or by Sondgard himself, and cheaper-looking cars with out-of-date licence plates were watched carefully, and the town's one motel was under constant surveillance, because all that money out around the lake inevitably drew thieves. Suspicious-looking types who could prove no legitimate reason for being in town were sent packing, with a warning not to come back.

And there was occasional trouble from the estates themselves. Four summers ago, a jumpy private guard with an itchy trigger finger had fired three shots into a car moving on one of the private roads, thinking it contained burglars. Later, he swore he'd called at the driver of the car to stop, and had fired only when the driver had ignored him. But the car had contained a pair of college kids, employed for the summer at Black Lake Lounge out by the summer theatre, off looking for a secluded place to neck, and not realizing this was a private road. When a uniformed man had shouted at them, the boy had panicked and had kept going, trying to drive away from there. One of the bullets fired at the car struck the boy in the head, killing him instantly.

So there were complicated times in the job, and messy times.

But all in all Sondgard was satisfied. The work was a pleasant contrast to the sedentary indoor life he spent the rest of the year, and it kept him busy, kept him from brooding about himself. If it weren't for the nagging of Joyce Ravenfield ...

But that was another subject entirely. Shying away from it, Sondgard forced himself to concentrate on what the radio was saying. The radio said, 'Extra margin because . . . ' and while Captain Sondgard drove, Professor Sondgard winced.

The flame-red of the summer theatre shone through the trees long before he'd come around the last curve and turned off on the gravel parking lot. Just ahead, across the road on the lake side, was the Black Lake Lounge, the only commercial property anywhere along the lake frontage. There was an extensive gambling setup on the second floor of the Lounge, and everyone knew it, but Sondgard also knew he wasn't supposed to do anything about it. His conscience wasn't particularly troubled, nor was his integrity very outraged; no paupers were cleaned of their last pfennigs upstairs in the Black Lake Lounge. It was a rich man's game up there, and no credit was given any player, so it was essentially harmless. The only police business that ever came out of the Lounge was the occasional drunken driver.

Sondgard parked the Volvo in front of the theatre, seeing the shiny blue-and-white prowl car already there. So Mike Tompkins already had arrived.

Sondgard went into the theatre first, and saw Mary Ann McKendrick behind the ticket window. She looked frightened, and her eyes were puffy, as though she'd been crying. She said, 'Next door, Mr Sondgard. In the house.'

'Thanks.'

He went next door, and found Mike Tompkins in the rehearsal room, standing by the door. A dozen or more people, men and women, were sitting in a stunned silence on the folding chairs. None of them met his eyes as he came in, nor were any of them looking at one another. They gazed at the floor, or at the ceiling, or over toward the window, and they all had the tightness of shock on their faces.

Sondgard recognized a few of them. Bob Haldemann, producer of the theatre. Loueen Campbell and Richard Lane and

Alden March, who'd acted here in other years, and Ralph Schoen the director, and Arnie Kapow the set designer. The others were all strangers to him.

Bob Haldemann finally got to his feet, saying, 'Hallo, Eric. I'm glad you're here.'

'In a minute, Bob. Mike?' He motioned to Mike Tompkins to come outside with him.

Mike Tompkins, bearing the rank of sergeant in the Cartier Isle police force, was a huge man, six foot, five inches tall, weighing nearly two hundred and sixty pounds, and none of it fat. A local boy, born and bred in Cartier Isle, he'd left his home town twice, the first time to accept a football scholarship at a Midwestern university – he'd flunked out the second semester of his sophomore year – and the second time to join the Marines. He'd spent twenty years in the Marines, which he enjoyed more than either college or football, and retired at thirty-nine, coming back home to live with his Japanese wife, May. Now forty-four, he looked barely thirty, and was an exercise-and-health-food nut. He was also mainly responsible for the police force's high ammunition bill each year, since he spent a part of nearly every day out on the practice range. He'd taken over the police force job three years ago, when the earlier sergeant – Crawford, his name was – retired, and since then he'd revamped the force completely. He and May designed the new uniform, a modified version of Marine dress uniform in a lighter shade of blue, and he also talked Mayor Ravenfield into trading in the force's seven-year-old Chevy station wagon for a brand-new blue-and-white Ford V8 with a red dome light. He enjoyed the uniform and the car and the chance at unlimited use of the practice range, but he usually ignored the job itself as much as possible. His relief at Sondgard's presence now was obvious and unashamed.

He and Sondgard stepped out to the hallway, and Sondgard shut the door before saying, 'You get the story?'
one in the world who knew Sondgard and called him Captain.
'I did. It's a mess, Captain, a real mess.' Mike was the only
'There really was a murder, then.'
'There sure was. She's upstairs.'

58

'A woman?'

'Girl. One of the actresses here. Looks like one of those sex maniac jobs.'

Sondgard looked toward the stairs. Would it be considered necessary for him to go up and view the body? He hoped not. What good could he do? He said, 'You better call in to Joyce. Tell her to notify Doc Walsh.'

'I did already.'

'All right. Good.' He looked at the staircase again. Wasn't there something else he should do? He said, 'Who discovered it?'

'Fella named Mel Daniels. Actor.'

'All right. I guess I want to talk to him first.'

'You want me to call Captain Garrett.'

Yes, he did, very much. Let Captain Garrett go up those stairs. But some embarrassment connected with Joyce Ravenfield made him say, 'Not yet. Let's get our facts straight first.'

'Okay, Captain.'

Sondgard went back into the rehearsal room. 'Bob,' he said, 'is there any place I can use for my interrogations?'

Haldemann got to his feet, looking eager to help. 'Well, I guess the kitchen,' he said. 'I guess that'd be the best. Unless you want to go over to the theatre. You could use my office over there.'

'No, the kitchen's fine. That's okay, Bob, I know where it is.' He looked around the room. 'Mel Daniels?'

An ashen-faced boy got shakily to his feet. Early twenties, wearing wrinkled slacks and a short-sleeved white shirt. It was Professor Sondgard who catalogued him: class comic, a facile learner, fifty-per-cent effort in his studies, occasionally in trouble with the Dean's office for being involved in panty raids or illegal bonfires on the main square in town or the painting of white bucks on the statue of the school founder. It was Captain Sondgard who said to him, 'Would you come with me, please?'

He led the way back out to the hall, and said to Mike Tompkins, 'When Doc Walsh comes, have him go right on upstairs. Keep the rest of them in there, and I'll talk to them one at a time.'

'Right. You want the recorder?'

'Oh, yes. Good idea.'

Sondgard and Mel Daniels went down the hallway to the kitchen, and sat down across from one another at the kitchen table. Sondgard brought out his cigarettes and offered one to the boy, who took it gratefully. Sondgard said, 'Pretty much of a shock, eh?'

'No encores, please.' The boy smiled shakily, and accepted a light.

Mike Tompkins came in with the Wollensack tape recorder from the prowl car, another of his innovations since joining the force. Mike loved gadgets, loved machinery, loved to be surrounded by things with motors and gears and levers and things that went whirr. He plugged the recorder in, put a fresh five-inch tape on, set the speed for three and three-quarter ips, positioned the microphone on its little stand midway between the two at the table, and said. 'All set, Captain.'

'Thanks, Mike.'

Mike went back out to stand guard in the hallway, and Sondgard switched the machine on. Feeling slightly foolish, he intoned, 'Preliminary questioning in the killing of – Oh, damn.' He switched the machine off again. 'What was her name?'

'Cissie. Uh, Cissie. I forget her last name.'

'Hold on.'

Sondgard went to the doorway and called to Mike, 'What was her name?'

'I don't know.'

'Ask somebody.'

Mike opened the rehearsal-room door and asked somebody, then passed the name on to Sondgard: 'Cissie Walker.'

'Cissie's a nickname.'

'Just a second.' He asked again, and said, 'Cynthia. Cynthia Walker.'

Songard went back to the kitchen table, put the tape back at the beginning, and started again: 'Preliminary questioning in the killing of Cynthia Walker. Four fifty-seven p.m., June 6th. First witness, Melvin – Is that right? Melvin?'

'Yes.'

'Melvin Daniels.'

'Actually, that's just my stage name. Mel Daniels. Do you want my legal name?'

Sondgard looked at him. The tape was going around, and somewhere upstairs a girl lay murdered, and Sondgard sat in this kitchen ensnarled in farce. They were doing a comedy routine, all of them, playing one long senseless gag on names. This was no place for Eric Sondgard. He should have called Garrett right away, no matter what Joyce might say or think.

But he was in it now, he had to keep going. He said. 'The stage name is good enough.' Anything to end the comedy. 'You were the one who found her, is that right?'

'Yes, sir.'

'Tell me about it.'

'Mr Haldemann told me to go upstairs and pick out a room. All the rooms were occupied on the second floor, so I went up to the third floor. I was trying the doors, looking for one that wasn't locked, because all the rooms that were already taken are kept locked. So her – door wasn't locked. I went in and saw her, and then I got sick, and then I ran downstairs and shouted for help. Mr Schoen, he's the director, he went upstairs to check, because I wouldn't go back up there again, and then he called the police.'

'And when was the last time you saw Miss Walker alive?'

'When I got here, this afternoon.'

'You just arrived this afternoon?'

'I'm a day late. There was a party for me and –'

'All right. What time was this, when you saw Miss Walker alive?'

'Around quarter to four, I guess. I came in on the bus at three o'clock, and Mary Ann McKendrick came down to town and picked me up at about three-thirty, maybe twenty-five minutes past three, and we drove out here, and that's when I met her.'

'Miss Walker.'

'That's right.'

'Then that was the only time you ever saw her alive?'

'Yes, sir.'

'And how did she act? Did she seem frightened of anything, or worried about anything?'

'No, sir. She – well, she flirted with me a little.'

'All right.' Sondgard took time out to light a cigarette of his own, and to think of what his next question should be. Probably it would be best to get a complete timetable from everybody.

Was the killer one of those people in the rehearsal room?

Oh, this was ridiculous. Sondgard had never met a killer in his life. He couldn't imagine what a killer would look like, or sound like. How could he seriously suspect *anyone?* No one looked like a killer to him.

It didn't have to be any of the people in the theatre company. Someone could have come in from outside.

Still, a timetable would be a good idea. He'd have something to turn over to Captain Garrett when the time came. So he said, 'All right, now, I'd like to get a complete rundown on your movements this afternoon, from the time you saw Miss Walker alive at three forty-five till you found her dead at – what time, about?'

'Four-thirty.'

'All right, forty-five minutes. Oh, by the way, where was Miss Walker when you first saw her?'

'Over in the theatre. In the box office.'

'That was at three forty-five. Now, what did you do next?'

Daniels gave a complete rundown of the next forty-five minutes. Since Haldemann had been showing him around the theatre, introducing him to the rest of the people in the company, Daniels could also give partial information on the whereabouts of nearly everyone else in the group at one time or another in those forty-five minutes. Sondgard heard him out, and though it was all going down on the tape he jotted some of it in his notebook just the same. He thought it might be helpful when he talked to the others if he had Daniels' timetable where he could refer to it instantly.

When Daniels was finished, Sondgard's notes read:

3 : 00 arr. in town
3 : 25 picked up by Mary Ann
3 : 40 arr. at theatre, meets dead girl in box office
3 : 40 – 4 : 05 in Bob H's office
4 : 05 – 4 : 25 meets Perry Kent and Arnie Kapow, both in
     theatre, meets two girls, Linda and Karen, washing flats
     back of theatre
4 : 25 meets Ralph Schoen and other members of company
     in rehearsal room. Not sure how many present.
4 : 30 find body. Saw no one in halls or on stairs.

Sondgard thanked Daniels for his cooperation and told him,
'Tell the sergeant I want to see Bob Haldemann next. And wait
in the rehearsal room, please.' Because Captain Garrett might
want to question everybody all over again. Sondgard couldn't
guess how many important questions he hadn't thought to ask.

Haldemann came in and confirmed Daniels' timetable, as he
had been with the boy from three-forty on. He and Daniels had
parted on the first-floor hall of this house just before Daniels
found the body. Haldemann had already gone back to the
office, and Will Henley, one of the actors, had come over to get
him after Ralph Schoen had checked and found Cissie Walker
really murdered.

As to the dead girl: 'She was a very cheerful girl, Eric.
Something of a flirt, I guess, but she didn't mean anything by
it.'

'Could someone have misunderstood, thought she *did* mean
something by it?'

'I don't see how. It was all too innocent and playful. She
was only nineteen, just being playful. I don't think anyone
could have thought she was serious about it all. She was
just – I don't know exactly how to explain it, Eric. She was
just a healthy, happy girl, having a lot of fun with the brand-
new discovery she was a woman. I wouldn't be surprised if
she were a virgin. In fact, I'd be surprised if she *weren't*.'

He could add nothing more. The dead girl, like the rest of
the company, had only been here since yesterday. So far as he
knew, no one else in the company had known Cissie Walker

before meeting her here. So far as he knew, no one had become a special friend or a special enemy of the girl in the twenty-four hours the company had been together.

Sondgard asked him, 'Is everybody in the company in that room out there?'

'All except Mary Ann; she's at the box office. And Tom Burns. You remember him, our stage manager. I imagine he's over at the Lounge. I haven't seen him since this morning.'

Sondgard remembered Tom Burns. So far as anyone knew, Burns hadn't drawn a sober breath in ten years. He was precise and competent and reliable as a stage manager, but whenever he was neither working nor sleeping he was drinking.

Sondgard said, 'Okay. I'll look for Tom later. Here' – he passed his notebook and pen across the table – 'make me a list of this year's company.'

Haldemann did. Including himself, there were fifteen names on the list. Sondgard looked at the list and shook his head. He'd be hours questioning all these people. He sighed and said, 'All right, I'll talk to Arnie next.'

But the questioning didn't take as long as he'd expected. Arnie Kapow had spent the entire afternoon in the scene dock in the theatre, and Perry Kent had spent the entire afternoon on the stage, setting up the lights. Neither of them knew anything about the killing. Nor could either of them be involved; they were alibied. In later questioning. Sondgard established that the theatre's front door had been under the eyes of Mary Ann McKendrick constantly between three-forty and four-thirty, and the rear door had been right next to where two of the young actresses, Linda Murchieson and Karen Leacock, had been washing flats. They had seen no one during that hour except Mel Daniels and Bob Haldemann.

After Arnie and Perry, Sondgard talked to Ralph Schoen, who was even fatter this year than last year. Schoen had spent the entire afternoon in the rehearsal room on the first floor. The doors to the hall had been closed, so anyone could have come into the house without being seen. Schoen could vouch for Loueen Campbell and Richard Lane, who had been doing most of the rehearsing and neither of whom had left the room at any time. He thought all of the others had stepped out at one time or another during the afternoon, but he couldn't be sure of specific times.

Loueen Campbell and Dick Lane, questioned after Schoen, merely agreed with what Schoen said, and could add nothing.

Alden March was the only other actor who'd been here before this summer. Sondgard knew him as he knew the others, because he'd developed the habit a few years ago of stopping by this house late at night, after a performance, to have a cup of coffee in the kitchen here with Bob and Ralph and the actors. For the last few years, Sondgard's summer nights had been spiced by good-humoured rehashings of the old argument about the actor's artistic status: Is an actor an artist, or is he simply the interpreter of the artistry of the playwright, as a musician is an interpreter of the artistry of the composer? But aren't some musicians artists in their own right? Aren't the most accomplished actors artists in their own right? And what about directors? And so on, and so on.

Alden March came into the kitchen now and looked around, smiling sadly. 'Not the usual joyous occasion, Eric,' he said. 'But I'm glad to see you nonetheless.'

That Alden was homosexual was no secret. But he kept his opinions to himself, and never strove to press his conviction on males who were not of his persuasion, so there was never any trouble over him. He even managed to spend his summers sharing a room with Tom Burns – who combined perpetual drunkenness with a well-developed lust that verged on satyriasis, totally female-directed – with no problems.

He was not obviously effeminate, with the pseudo-girlish posturing associated with the homosexual. He was, in fact, very masculine in both looks and manner, which had caused more than one woman to offer him her all in a missionary attempt to show him the error of his ways. The missionaries, so far, had all failed.

He had nothing to add to what Sondgard had already learned. He had spent the afternoon in the rehearsal room. He'd stepped out of the room for about five minutes somewhere between two-thirty and three o'clock, and he vaguely remembered others making similar brief trips, but he couldn't be precise about times. He'd been concentrating totally on the rehearsal.

After Alden, Sondgard took a break, to go through what he'd been told and see if there was anything of importance he'd overlooked. He had so far questioned eight people. Of them, six had alibis; Arnie Kapow and Perry Kent in the theatre, Ralph Schoen and Loueen Campbell and Dick Lane in the rehearsal room, Bob Haldemann with Mel Daniels. Daniels really should be considered a non-suspect, too, but Sondgard hesitated to eliminate him. It was remotely possible that Daniels had killed her himself, and then had made a big show of discovering the body. Had there been time enough? Haldemann had left him, he'd gone upstairs, he'd come running back down stairs all in about five minutes. Could he have committed a murder in those five minutes? Unlikely. So he was a possibility, but far from a probability.

And the same was true of Alden March. Alden might actually have left the rehearsal room an hour later than he'd claimed. He had no rock-solid alibi. But Alden was even more unlikely than Daniels, if this was actually a sex killing.

So out of the eight, Sondgard had six impossibles and two improbables. And there was still the strong possibility that it was none of these people at all, but a stranger from outside.

Well, he would try to be dispassionate about this. He would assume, for the moment, that the killer was one of these fifteen people on the list Bob had made for him. Six were eliminated, two were almost eliminated. That left seven, four men and three women. If it was a sex killing, the list was cut to four. Three actors and one stage manager. Ken Forrest, Will Henley, Rod McGee, and Tom Burns.

Sondgard stalled. He sent next for Linda Murchieson and Karen Leacock, who simply verified the earlier statements, and neither of whom had seen any strangers slinking around anywhere. Now only Mary Ann McKendrick was left, and the four men.

Mary Ann McKendrick.

For the last hour and a half, alone in the theatre.

'Don't you have any *sense?*' He said it aloud, irritating himself further.

But what kind of stupidity was it, when one girl had been murdered, to let another girl stay all alone in an empty theatre? If he'd heard of anyone else doing it, he would have said the man in charge was an imbecile.

The man in charge. The whole problem was that *he* was the man in charge, but he didn't *feel* like the man in charge. He was just making motions like a police captain, salving his pride for an hour or two before calling Captain Garrett in. Captain Garrett was actually the man in charge; it was just that Captain Garrett didn't know it yet.

Sondgard hurried to the doorway, and called, 'Mike! Get over to the theatre, and tell Mary Ann to come back here. You know she's over there alone?'

'Son of a bitch!' Mike stormed away, his boots booming heavy across the porch and down the stoop.

Sondgard remained in the doorway, waiting, half fearful that Mike would come back alone, to tell him his blundering had ended in another death. But when the front door opened again, Mike came in with Mary Ann, and Sondgard smiled with relief. 'Down here, Mary Ann,' he called. 'You too, Mike.'

They both came down the hallway toward him. Sondgard said, 'Just sit down at the table there, Mary Ann. Mike, go on over to the Lounge, see if Tom Burns is there. If he is, send him back here, tell him to come straight in to see me. And you stick around, find out has he been there steadily all afternoon. Get his movements particularly between three-thirty and four-thirty.'

'Right.'

Sondgard went back to the table, sat down, and started the recorder again. The first five-inch reel was full by now, and they were halfway through one side of the second reel. Joyce Ravenfield could type up an extract of the important parts tonight. She needn't copy the whole thing, at least not right away.

Sondgard had very few questions to ask the girl. She simply substantiated Mel Daniels' story, confirmed the fact that neither

Perry Kent nor Arnie Kapow had left the theatre by the front door, and verified Bob Haldemann's statement that he had come right back to the theatre at four-thirty, after leaving Daniels at the house.

She did have one additional piece of information: 'When I brought Mel Daniels up from town, Cissie was in the box office. She asked me to take over for her for a while. She had tight loafers on, and they were bothering her; she wanted to go change into sneakers.'

'This was at three-forty.'

'I guess so. Right around there. Just when I got here with Mel Daniels.'

'So she left the theatre at three-forty, to go over to the house. Did she meet anybody outside, or say anything about planning to meet anybody?'

'She didn't say anything, no. Just that she wanted to change her shoes. And I didn't see anybody out in front of the theatre at all.'

'Didn't you get a little worried when she didn't come back for so long?'

She fidgeted, and looked embarrassed. 'We shouldn't speak unkindly of the dead,' she said, somewhat prim. 'But Cissie didn't seem very . . . reliable. It honestly didn't surprise me that she left me there for nearly an hour.'

'All right. Thanks, Mary Ann. I'd like you to wait awhile, if you can. You can phone your mother if you want. Just wait in the rehearsal room with the others.'

'Somebody has to be in the box office, to answer the phone.'

'Have Bob do it. Or he can send one of the men I've already talked to. Not one of the girls.'

'Oh. Yes, I see. All right.'

As she was leaving the kitchen, Tom Burns came in. In his late thirties, he was about five foot nine and somewhat gone to seed, with a pronounced paunch and sagging shoulders. His face had an unhealthy red complexion, and his hair was a dry and sandy brown, thinning on top.

He was, of course, drunk. No more drunk than usual, and no less. Drunkenness in Tom showed only in the slow care of his walk and movements and speech, and a slight fuzziness in his eyes as though he couldn't focus as well as most people. He came in now, saying, 'Summertime! It is now officially summertime, our official has arrived. It's good to see you, Eric.'

'The official is here on official business, Tom. Didn't Mike tell you?'

'Michael Tompkins never tells me anything. One time, if memory serves, Michael Tompkins said to me, and I quote, quote, I wish I had you in my outfit, Burns, for just one week, I'd make a man of you, unquote. Prior to that threat, and also post to that threat, Michael Tompkins has never said anything to me at all. May I sit down?'

'I wish you would.'

Burns sat down at the table, as carefully as though sitting on eggs. 'He did, howsomever, tell me just now to come over here and look for you in the kitchen. I did, and I found you.'

'Were you over at the Lounge all afternoon, Tom?'

'What's that, a tape recorder?'

'Yes. Were you?'

Burns frowned, his mobile face going into contortions to achieve the expression. He said, 'Serious, Eric? Is this really something serious?'

'A girl was murdered here this afternoon, Tom.'

'Murdered? For God's sake, Eric! One of *our* girls? Who?'

'Her name was Cissie Walker.'

'Walker. Cissie Walker.' Burns twisted his face around some more, this time to show concentration. His face worked like faces in silent comedies, exaggerating all expressions into parodies of themselves. He had a small but bushy moustache, the same dry sandy brown as his hair, which added to the effect.

'Cissie Walker,' he repeated. 'Now, which one is that? We've only been together since yesterday, you know, there's three new ones. Wait a minute. The buxom blonde?'

'I don't know. I've never seen her.'

'Cissie . . . Sure, that's which one. Fantastic, Eric, absolutely fantastic. A Rubens nude. Stacked, overflowing, an abundance of riches. A rump like a mare, Eric. Pearl-white boobies like great white pillows.'

'I said she was killed, Tom.'

'Oh!' His eyes widened, and his hands went to his mouth, as though to block it before he could say anything more. 'I didn't even *think*. Oh my God, Eric, what a way to talk! Eric, on my honour, I wasn't even *thinking*, I was just shooting off my mouth, you know the way I am.'

'All right, Tom.'

'Murdered, for God's sake. Who can accept a thing like that, right off the bat? You talk about a girl – I just saw her this morning at breakfast. She was really killed, Eric?'

'She really was.'

'Christ, what a shame. I mean that, Eric, you know I do. A young girl like that, what a shame. What a waste. Gahh, there I go again!'

Burns really did seem more shaken and disoriented than Sondgard had ever seen him before, but Sondgard could understand why. Whatever it was about the world that troubled Burns, he had years ago chosen drink as the antidote. He kept himself anesthetized with liquor, so he would never have to take anything seriously. But this, the murder of a young girl, was so strong and violent a fact that even Tom Burns couldn't drown it or blur its outlines. It was impinging on him with all its reality, and it had been too many years since Burns had had anything to do with uncushioned reality.

As much to help Burns get back on an even keel as to go on with the interview, Sondgard repeated his original question again: 'Were you at the Lounge all afternoon, Tom?'

'Well, sure. You know me. I've been hanging around over there since breakfast time. Watched the sailboats for a while. Got acquainted again with Henry, the bartender over there.'

'And you don't have any idea about this murder? No one who acted sore at the girl, or acted, uh ...'

'Hot for her? Eric, anybody who saw that girl would be hot for her. I didn't see anybody drooling down his chin, if that's what you mean.'

'I guess that's what I mean.'

'It was somebody here? Is that what it is, Eric?'

'I don't know yet. It could be.'

'What a shame, Eric. What a crying shame.'

Sondgard switched the recorder off again. He had nothing more to ask Tom Burns. He said, 'Will you wait with the others in the rehearsal room for a while? And send in . . .' He checked the list Bob Haldemann had made. 'Send in Ken Forrest.'

'Right. A real shame, Eric. You should have met her.'

Ken Forrest came in promptly. He looked to be in his middle twenties, about six feet tall, with crew-cut black hair and a solemn expression. Sondgard motioned at the chair across the table, and Forrest silently sat down. Sondgard switched on the tape recorder and intoned, 'Preliminary questioning of Ken Forrest. Is that Kenneth?'

'Yes, sir.' His voice was soft, almost inaudible. He watched Sondgard intently, his eyes never shifting a second.

'Speak a little louder, please.'

'I'm sorry, sir. Yes, my name is Kenneth.'

'And your permanent address?'

'Three Ninety-two West Fifteenth Street, New York City. Apartment Three-B.'

'This is your first year at this theatre, is it not?'

'Yes, sir.'

'Could you give me a brief history of yourself up till this year? You understand, I don't know you yet. Most of the people here I do know, and the rest of you I want to know.'

'Yes, sir. You think it was one of us.'

'I think that's possible, yes.'

'A brief history, you say, sir. I was born in Lincoln, Nebraska, and lived there till I was nineteen. Then I enlisted in the Army and spent three years there, mostly in Japan. After my discharge I went to New York. Three years ago, that was. I've worked at a number of jobs, mostly clerical work, and I've attended drama classes. I've had small parts in two off-Broadway productions, and I was in the national touring company of *Love Among the Falling Stars*. Last summer I was with the Keelsville Players in Maine. I got my Equity card there, and that's how I happened to be eligible for the touring company.'

'Why didn't you go back to the theatre in Maine this summer?'

'They went bankrupt last year, sir.'

'I see. Have you ever been in any trouble with the police of any kind? I mean, besides parking tickets, things like that.'

Forrest's lips stretched in a small tight smile. 'Not even parking tickets, sir. I've never been in trouble of any kind.'

'All right. Now, this afternoon. You were in the rehearsal room, is that right?'

'Yes, sir, I was.'

'Did you leave the room at any time?'

'Yes, sir. Around three o'clock, I think, I went upstairs to the bathroom.'

'How long were you gone?'

'Five or ten minutes.'

'This was around three o'clock.'

'Yes, sir. I'm sorry, I can't pinpoint it exactly.'

'That's all right. Did you notice, did anyone else leave the room at any time?'

'Oh, yes, sir. Most of us did, in fact. But if you want to know who left at what time, I'm afraid I couldn't be of much help. I was watching Mr Schoen, most of the time. The director is vitally important in any sort of theatrical undertaking. He and he alone determines whether it will be a good production with well-behaved actors and a feeling of high morale within the group, or a bad production with ill-behaved actors and a feeling of low morale with warring cliques. So I was watching Mr Schoen, to see what sort of summer I could expect.'

'Oh? And what did you decide?'

'I really don't think it will be a particularly good summer, sir.'

That was all he had to offer. Sondgard asked him a few more questions, but with no result. He had seen no strangers hanging around the area, he had seen no one take a particular interest in Cissie Walker, he had not noticed any apprehension in Cissie Walker's manner the last time he saw her alive, this morning at breakfast.

Will Henley was next. He was a stocky man who looked to be about thirty, five foot, ten inches tall, with a heavy face that could become Shakespeare's Falstaff or Hammett's Casper Gut-

man with equal aptitude. He was wearing brown slacks and
tan polo shirt, the shirt stretched tight across heavy chest and
heavier stomach. He sat down, and Sondgard announced the
normal preliminary statement, then asked, 'Your permanent
address?'

'One Ninety-two West Seventy-second Street, New York.'

'This is your first season here?'

'If there is a season here, yes.' There was a note of heavy
irritation in Henley's voice; at the moment he was being more
Gutman than Falstaff.

'What do you mean by that?'

'This – All right if I smoke?'

'Go ahead.'

Sondgard waited while Henley took his time lighting a cigarette. He wondered if this was Henley's normal manner, or was
he trying to be offensive because Sondgard was a cop, or was he
just regretting his choice of a summer job.

When Henley finally got the cigarette going and still didn't
say anything, Sondgard repeated his question: 'What do you
mean, *if* there's a season?'

'We're supposed to open in a week and a half. If you don't
solve this killing by then, will you let us open?'

'Why not?'

Henley shrugged. 'All right,' he said, as though tabling that
subject for the moment. 'What if there's more killings?'

'Do you think there will be?'

Henley nodded his head toward the front of the house. '*They*
think so.'

'Why?'

'A maniac doesn't just kill once. You think it's one of us, don't
you?'

'Not necessarily.'

'*They* think it is.'

'Do you?'

Henley shrugged again, tabling another topic. 'Besides,' he
said, 'they're already talking about getting away from here.'

'The other actors?'

'The whole crowd. Nobody wants to be next.'

Sondgard found himself getting irritated. There was in Henley's manner some sort of implication that Sondgard couldn't be relied upon to do much in this case, that the people here were pretty much on their own. Sondgard was constantly reminding himself of his lack of competence and experience in something like this, but he didn't like the same sort of reminder coming from someone else.

He failed to hide his own irritation as he said, 'We'll do our best to see that nobody *is* next. To begin with, I'd like to get back to the interview.'

As usual, Henley's answer was a shrug. His whole manner seemed to be that he didn't expect to be disappointed by Sondgard since he wasn't looking for much from Sondgard anyway.

Sondgard said, 'First, I want you to give me a brief auto-biography. Jobs you've had, places you've lived.'

'Of course.' And even in that brief phrase, there was something vaguely insulting. Henley reached out and flicked ashes from his cigarette, then leaned back in the chair and gazed at the ceiling as he recited: 'I was born in Boston, and grew up here and there around the world. My father's an Army officer. He wanted me to go to West Point, but one childhood on Army bases is enough. On my eighteenth birthday, I enlisted, and that took care of that. My father will never forgive me for having been an enlisted man. When I got out, on my twenty-first birthday, I went to L.A. I got my discharge in Texas, and it didn't matter where I went, so I went to L.A. I hung around there for a year, and met a few actors, and got interested in acting. But the big goal out there is to get your own Western series, and that's just the Army all over again. So I went to New York. I've been in four plays, all off-Broadway and three small television parts, one of them in a soap opera, and I was in a crowd scene in a movie, and I had a small part in a commercial. I was one member of a football team, running around throwing this box of cereal to each other. Summer before last, I was at Tent Theatre in Pillicoke, Pennsylvania. Last summer, I was with the Dark Horse Players in Estes Park, Colorado. That's near Denver. And this summer I'm here.'

'You never spend more than one summer at the same theatre?'

'Why should I? A different vacation every summer.'

'I see. And what do you do for a living, in New York, when you're not acting?'

'I collect unemployment insurance.'

'Do you attend drama classes?'

'No. That stuff's a farce. Makework for losers.'

Again it was Professor Sondgard rather than Captain Sondgard who analyzed and typed this boy. He was another common type on college campuses: arrogant and opinionated, but with the quick mind and facile ability to back up his boasting with performance. This type usually had only the resilence and adaptability of youth to rely on, and once youth was gone they were bereft and bitter.

With less irritation, now that he had placed Henley, Sondgard asked him, 'How old are you now?'

'Twenty-seven.'

So he had a few years left before the decline. He was welcome to them. Sondgard glanced at his notes and asked, 'Have you ever had any trouble with the police? Aside from parking tickets and things like that.'

'Drunk and disorderly one time in L.A.,' said Henley carelessly. 'A bunch of us had a party down at the beach. It got a little out of hand.'

'That's all?'

'That's all.'

'All right. Now, about this afternoon. You were at the rehearsal.'

'If you could call it that.'

Sondgard raised an eyebrow. 'You didn't care for it?'

'Paid amateurs,' said Henley.

'Today was the first day of rehearsals, wasn't it?'

'You don't need to smell a rotten egg for an hour to know it's bad.'

'Well, never mind about that. You were at the rehearsal. Did you leave the room at any time?'

'Of course. It was a waste of time for most of us to be there

75

anyway. Campbell and Lane were doing all the rehearsing.'

'What time did you leave?'

'Around two-thirty.'

'And how long were you gone?'

'Maybe fifteen, twenty minutes. I went upstairs and had a cigarette.'

'So you got back to the room around quarter to three.'

'Roughly.'

'Roughly, yes. Do you remember any of the others leaving the rehearsal at any time during the afternoon?'

'Sure. They all did, sooner or later. It wasn't what you'd call an inspired afternoon.'

'Did anyone leave *after* your smoke break?'

Henley shrugged. 'I don't know, I suppose so. I wasn't paying much attention.'

'But you weren't concentrating on the rehearsal either. What were you thinking about?'

'New York. I should have stayed there this summer.' His sudden smile was surprisingly open and pleasant. 'I knew it even before that girl got herself killed.'

'Got herself killed?'

'You never saw her in action, huh?'

'No.'

'She kept throwing it around. So somebody made the catch.'

'Did she throw it toward you?'

Will Henley's smile this time was mocking. 'I wear pants,' he said. 'That means she did. But it doesn't mean I killed her. I don't have to kill them.'

'All right,' said Sondgard, wondering what Joyce would think of that when she came to it in the transcribing. 'I guess that's all. Send Rod McGee in, will you?'

'Sure.' Henley got to his feet, and Sondgard could see why he'd been cast as a football player in that commercial. Although he wasn't particularly tall – around five eight – there was a massive quality to him. At first he seemed fat, but it wasn't fat. Will Henley was solid, and probably very strong.

Henley left the room, and a minute later Rod McGee came in. The contrast between the two was complete. McGee was thin as a rail, with a wiry look to him, and he seemed to radiate nervous energy, as though he would make a spark if you touched him. And as Will Henley looked somewhat older than his twenty-seven years, Rod McGee surely looked younger than he really was. He had a bony and unlovely face, with strikingly bright brown eyes, and the eager open expression of a teenager. He looked to be no more than nineteen or twenty.

He came over and bounced down on to the chair. 'Is that a Wollensack?' His quick fingers tapped the tape recorder.

'Yes.'

'An old one, or one of the new ones?'

'I don't know how old it is.'

'It was a better machine before, when the German company owned it. Now it's a subsidiary of Revere. Did you know that?'

'No,' I didn't. What is Rod short for? Robert?'

'No, my name is Fredric, and then it went to Fred, and then it went to Rod.'

'All right. Excuse me a second.' He started the machine and said, 'Preliminary question of Fredric McGee, known as Rod McGee. How old are you, Rod?'

'Twenty-six.'

'And your permanent address?'

'You want my folks', or where I live in New York?'

'Do you have a permanent address in New York?'

'Yeah, 37A Carmine Street.'

'Have you been employed at this theatre before this summer?'

'No, never. I just got here yesterday. First time I've ever been in this part of the country at all. I like it.'

'Good. Now, please, give me a brief autobiography. Where you've lived, what jobs you've held, your theatrical background.'

'Oh, well, let me see. You want addresses?'

'No, just the city, and during what period you lived there.'

'Well, let me see. Albany, New York, to begin with. I mean, I was born there. And grew up there. I had part-time jobs when I was a kid . . . do you want those?'

'No, not particularly.'

'Well, then, when I got out of high school, I went to – Oh. You want the name of the high school?'

'It isn't your childhood I'm mainly interested in.'

'Oh. Well . . . College?'

'You went to college?'

'Yes, sir, sure. Monequois College, Monequois, New York. Drama and American Lit., combined major. Then I was drafted – right after I got out of college, I mean. I was drafted, and I went to Texas for basic training and then to New Jersey, and then to Rhode Island. Then when I got out, I went to New York to take drama classes. I had this introduction from my drama teacher at Monequois to Jule Kemp. The teacher, you know. And I studied with him ever since.'

'Have you had professional acting jobs?'

'Well, Jule doesn't like the students to do that, you know, but I did get a couple of jobs. I was in a show on weekends, for children, on Saturday and Sunday afternoon. I was the Foolish Knight; I get lost, and eat the poisoned apple, and all sorts of things. And I got a couple of daytime television jobs; I was on a soap opera for three weeks once – I was this Army buddy of this character, he brings me home from camp and there's all this trouble – and I was in a skit on a quiz show. I dressed up in an Arab costume, and I meet Death, and he talks to me, and the answer was *Appointment in Samarra*.'

'Are you in Actor's Equity?'

'Oh, sure. I apprenticed two summers ago at Southern Tier Playhouse in Binghamton, New York.'

'Why didn't you go back there this summer?'

'Oh. Well, it doesn't have a repertory company like this, you know, it's all package shows. The year I was there we had Tallulah Bankhead and Arthur Treacher and Victor Jory and –'

'All right, fine. What about last summer?'

'Oh, I stayed in New York last summer. I had this very good job with a suntan-lotion company. *Bronzo*, it's called. I went around to five-and-tens and department stores and everything, and I put on displays for this suntan lotion. It was pretty good lotion, too.'

78

'Have you had other jobs in New York, besides acting jobs?'

'Oh, sure. I worked for a moving company – you know, furniture movers. Scappali Brothers. And I work for the city every time there's a snowfall, you know, I shovel snow. And I had a job for a while at this settlement house on East Fifth Street, I taught drama to this bunch of kids, we put on *Our Town*. It was pretty good.'

'Good,' said Sondgard, smiling. The contrast between Rod McGee and Will Henley went deeper than physical appearance. Here was the eager boy, the willing worker, the one who in college wound up on every club's Entertainment Committee, who never got a single mark higher than B or lower than C, who loaned his money indiscriminately, and who at a get-together in a professor's home would leap to help the professor's wife with the refreshments. Not out of calculation, but simply because that's the way he was.

Sondgard asked the next question for the record only, expecting a negative answer. 'Have you ever been in trouble with the police? Parking tickets and such excepted.'

'Oh, no. Not till now. I mean – I guess I'm not really what you'd call in trouble now either, am I? But I mean I've never even *talked* to a policeman before, except maybe ask directions or something.'

'All right, fine. Now, this afternoon. You spent the entire time at the rehearsal, is that right?'

'Oh, sure. Listen, do you think we'll be able to go on? I mean, I know that sounds awfully heartless, with Cissie just dead and all, you know, but we've all been talking in there and we were kind of wondering, you know ...'

'I imagine the play will go on.' Sondgard smiled. 'The show *must* go on, remember?'

'Sure, I know. But a couple of us were thinking maybe it wouldn't. I don't know, I guess it doesn't make any difference.'

'Just a minute.' Sondgard was finding Rod McGee the most difficult of them all to interview. The boy kept going off on tangents, and it took a bulldozer to bring him back. 'About this afternoon,' Sondgard insisted. 'You say you spent *all* your time at the rehearsal?'

'Oh, sure. We started at – '

'Yes, I know what time you started.' But as soon as he said it, Sondgard was sorry, afraid he'd sounded harsh. Rod McGee was certainly friendly and cooperative, and it wasn't his fault if he was too eager to be orderly. More softly, Sondgard said, 'But I was wondering if you spent every minute in that room there. You didn't leave at all to – '

'Oh, to go to the bathroom!' It burst out of him, and he was sparkling again. 'Oh, sure! I'm sorry, honest, I didn't know what you meant. Oh, sure. I went to the bathroom twice.'

'What times?'

'A little after two, I guess, and maybe around three-thirty, quarter to four.'

'Did you see anyone else in the house either time?'

'No, I didn't. You think it was a prowler, huh?'

'It might have been.'

'Some of the others say you think it's one of us. That would be a real mess, wouldn't it?'

'Yes, it would. Now, did you happen to notice – '

But he never got to finish the sentence. Mike Tompkins stuck his head in the door at that moment and said, 'Captain, can I see you for a second?'

'What? Oh, yes. Be right with you.' He turned off the tape recorder and told Rod McGee, 'I guess that's all. Thank you for cooperating. Would you go back with the others now? Tell them I'll be with them in a minute.'

'Will do.' McGee got to his feet. He motioned at the tape recorder. 'That looks like one of the new ones,' he said.

Mike was waiting impatiently in the doorway, a strained expression on his face. Sondgard got up from the table and went over to him, saying, 'What is it, Mike?'

'Something I want to show you.'

Sondgard went with him, the two of them following Rod McGee down the hall. McGee went into the rehearsal room. Standing at the foot of the stairs, looking unusually pale, was Tom Burns.

Mike said, 'Tom here found it. None of the others know about it yet.'

'What is it?'

'You ought to see it for yourself. Come on along, Tom.'

'Anything to be of service,' said Burns, but he sounded reluctant.

The three men went upstairs, and Mike led the way to the bathroom. 'Here it is, Captain.'

Sondgard looked where Mike was pointing. On the mirror over the sink, in a huge and childish scrawl, were the words, I'M SORRY. The letters were shaky and ill-formed, sprawling over the entire surface of the mirror, the 'Y' of SORRY crammed against the edge of the mirror by the size of the letters preceding it. The writer had pressed the soap so hard against the mirror that chunks of it stuck here and there, protuberances on the letters, and more small pieces had dropped to the sink. The bar of soap itself, all mashed together, lay in the soap dish on the sink.

Sondgard looked at the letters, and felt a sudden rush of pity. A poor bewildered mind had scrawled out those words, and Sondgard had no doubt they were sincere. This creature, whoever he was, driven by whatever sickness infested his brain, had raped and killed. And then, in shock and terror and remorse, he had come here to gaze upon his own face in this mirror, and to scratch out on its surface his plea for forgiveness.

A madman. Not simply a low and cunning intelligence, or a brutish mind, but a sensitive mind twisted by madness. Just as Sondgard had placed and typed the people he had questioned, trying to understand them, now he automatically built up in his mind a portrait of this poor lost wretch, who here for the second time had left his spoor. If the carnage upstairs was the result of a Mr Hyde, this writing on the mirror was surely the outcry of a Dr Jekyll. It was Jekyll that Sondgard pitied, forced to share the same husk with Hyde.

Was that husk here in this house? Sondgard riffled the mental daguerreotype he had made of his suspects, and tried to match one up against the daguerreotype of this sick and twisted human being. But he couldn't find the pair that matched, and a paraphrase of a line from television ran idiotically through his head: *Will the real madman please stand?*

So, not yet. He would have to talk to them more, he would have to get to know them better.

Mike's usually loud voice was unexpectedly hushed. He said, 'You want me to call Captain Garrett now, Captain?'

Captain Garrett?

No, not this time. Captain Garrett was a hunter. This poor wretch couldn't be hunted; he would have to be understood. Would Captain Garrett, on seeing this pitiful message, have understood its implications as Sondgard did?

'Maybe there's prints on that soap,' said Mike, more to himself than Sondgard.

Of course. That's what Garrett would see. A clue to the man's hands, not a clue to his soul.

It was one of the people waiting in the room downstairs. Sondgard knew that now as surely as if the guilty man had come and whispered it in his ear. After the crime, coming down the stairs, he had stopped here to remove the evidences of what he had done. And why? To make himself presentable when he returned to the group below. And he had scrawled this message to whom? To his co-workers, pleading with them for understanding. A stranger from outside would not have left this message here. Either the message would have been found in the murdered girl's room itself, or it would have come through the mail – shaky block letters clipped from a newspaper.

The killer was here, in this house. Sondgard had talked to him. Sondgard would find him.

'Captain? You want me to call Captain Garrett?'

'No,' said Sondgard. 'Not yet. We'll handle it ourselves for a while.'

Externally, the asylum wore the modern look. Situated atop a clear and grassy knoll, it presented to the visitor a pleasing façade, the bright brick administration building fronted by white pillars and with an approach of white limestone-painted rocks bounding the asphalt road through well-landscaped and well-manicured lawn.

Behind the administration building were three other buildings, all the same two stories in height, and connected by covered walkways amid more landscaping. One of these buildings was the infirmary, where the physical sicknesses of the mentally ill were cared for. One housed the non-violent patients, those well enough to be allowed freely to walk the grounds; the doors of this building were never locked, and the rocking chairs on the veranda were full throughout these soft spring days. Only the third building, farthest back, most hidden from the sight of the casual visitor, bore the physical appearance of the stock asylum. Somehow, the brick of this building seemed dingier and darker. The windows were smaller, and all were heavily barred. The door was stout, and always locked. Spotlights at the corners of the roof gleamed down at night, washing over the walls and the near grounds.

Standing in his office in the administration building, Dr Edward Peterby gazed out his window at the maximum-security building. It was from that building that the madman had escaped, killing two male nurses on the way.

'He has a high degree of intelligence,' said Dr Peterby, still looking out the window. Behind him, the police officers and the newsmen shifted position, cleared their throats, made small noises. Dr Peterby nodded at the maximum-security building. 'No one has ever escaped from there before. We would have said it was impossible. But he did it. With a combination of great intelligence and a capability for direct incisive action, he managed to get away.'

Dr Peterby turned away from the window at last, and faced the roomful of men. 'Before his sickness,' he said, 'his IQ was rated at 168. That puts him in genius class. Economic pressures had forced him into a job that would have frustrated an IQ of 120. That was one of the reasons he eventually wound up here.'

Dr Peterby paused. He felt this was important, though he knew it wasn't the part these men had come to hear. But he wanted them to understand. 'This man,' he said, 'is more to be pitied than hated. I can say that although he has murdered at least five times that we know of, twice before being sent here, and three times on the way out. If we are to include the young man murdered by the hitchhiker.'

One of the police officers cleared his throat and said, 'We include him, Doctor. The timing is right, the method is right, the descriptions from the other drivers are right.'

'Well, then.' Dr Peterby sat down at his desk, spread his hands flat on the warm wood. This crowding of his office had unnerved him somewhat; extra chairs had been brought in, and the room was full of his visitors. He was used to the warmth and spaciousness of this office, and now it was cool and crowded, the coolness emanating from the cold faces of the police officers and newsmen. He was used to dimness and silence in this room, and now the overhead light was on – which it never was when he was in it; he only used the desk lamp, even at night – and there were constant small noises from the waiting group of men.

Dr Peterby made a tent, joining the fingertips of both hands together, analyzed it as symbolic of a desire to crawl away into a small dim place away from all these faces, and broke the tent apart. 'Well, then,' he said again. 'You all have photos of Robert Ellington; you know what he looks like. You know, to a certain extent, what he has done. Now, as I understand it, you want to know what he *is*, what sort of man he is, what we can expect him to do.'

He paused. They waited. He said, 'Robert Ellington is, as I said, a highly intelligent man. He is also an extremely cunning man, an admission which I make with some regret. He was not a cunning man when he came here. We strove to cure him when he first came here, and in so doing we were striving to force him to understand himself, and to understand the enormity of what he had done. To understand that he had been wrong, and that he had been wrong in a terrible and inhuman way. He resisted us, as of course he must. If he is to retain his own regard, his own self-respect, he cannot believe that his actions were anything less that proper and necessary and inevitable. When he came to us, he was a violent man, but an open man, revealing himself completely, revealing himself far more than he knew. But in our attempt to hold up a mirror before his gaze, to reflect back to him the insights he had given us about himself, we only succeeded in teaching him how to avoid giving us any more revelations. We underestimated him – more than once, as you can see; he got away – but we underestimated him, and we only made matters worse.'

Looking down, Dr Peterby saw that unconsciously he had made the tent again. He broke it at once, with a sudden feeling of irritation, and pressed his palms down on the desk top. Watching his hands, he said, 'It isn't easy to admit an error like that. It was a grievous error. Methods which had worked with varying success on other men were no good on Robert Ellington. We had not taken into account the strength and adaptability of his mind.'

He raised his head to look at his visitors once more. 'That is a vitally important point,' he said. 'The adaptability of his mind. The defences he is capable of erecting are utterly fantastic. He learned here to be a man of a thousand psychic faces. Until he grew violent again and had to be put in the solitary ward, he displayed an amazing ability at mimicry. I could play for you tape recordings of our sessions together during that time, and they would astonish you. He was never the same man twice. He would choose one of the other inmates, and very nearly *become* that person. His speech, his responses, his attitudes, all would reflect almost a parody of the original, with his own personality showing through only as a muted left hand, as it were, in a minor key. Do you see what he was doing? Ours was a doctor-patient relationship which he could not evade, but which he could not accept because it would inevitably lead to disclosure about himself which he did not want to know. So he *altered* the doctor-patient relationship by becoming one of my other patients. Whatever I said to him, it was that other patient who answered, and whatever revealing information I might unearth about the other patient, could certainly not harm him.'

Dr Peterby's hands fluttered, his face was animated. He had very nearly forgotten his disruption of his office. 'Do you see the fantastic implications of what he did? Great intelligence, great cunning, a high order of talent, all bent on this one goal. The potential of this man is very nearly unbelievable. Well, you can see that for yourselves. He managed to break out of our maximum-security building. Alone, penniless, his name and face and general whereabouts known to all of you, he nevertheless managed to evade you. If we could yet find the key to this man, break him from the bondage of his illness, unlock his potential, what a value he could be to society!'

'We have to find the man himself first,' said one of the police officers. 'And right now he isn't being a value to society, he's being a menace to society.'

'Yes. Yes. I know. He must be found, before he does even greater damage to himself. You must know, it is entirely possible that he will kill again. What these three killings have already done to him I can't begin to guess. The longer he remains free, the more difficult his eventual cure will become. All the time he is out there, he is piling up more and more data he must forever hide from himself; he is making the wall between himself and self-knowledge thicker and thicker and higher and higher.'

'He is also killing people.'

'Good God, I'm well aware of that! Do you think I'm *ignoring* that? The two men here, I knew them both, knew them for years. I would have said they were friends of mine, as much as there are friendships between the staff and the employees at ward level. One of them – Davis – I know his wife, I've met their children. Of *course* it's a dreadful thing, I know that as well as anyone. But it's dreadful in the way a flood is dreadful, in the way an airplane crash is dreadful. You don't *hate* the water, or *hate* the airplane, and if you do you're just being foolish and wasting your emotions. I realize this is a different situation here, Robert Ellington can hardly be considered an act of God, but –'

'More an act of Satan,' said one of the newsmen.

'Very well,' said Dr Peterby, nodding. 'Very well, if you want to phrase it that way. Robert Ellington is possessed by a devil, if you will, and we here are the priests trying to exorcise that devil. The devil, in this case, is a mental illness. Once Robert

Ellington is cured, if we ever do manage to cure him, he will be as shocked and repulsed at these crimes as you or I, and he will have just as strong a feeling as you or I that *he* was not the one who committed those crimes. I know *I* didn't murder those people. You know *you* didn't murder them. If and when he is ever healthy, he will know just as surely that *he* didn't murder them, and he will be right. It is the disease within him that is killing, not him. The law recognizes that fact. When caught, he will not be punished; he will be returned here. If cured, he will be released, and he will *still* not be punished. He will be a free man.'

Dr Peterby wasn't sure he was getting through to these people. But he knew he *had* to, if they were to know Robert Ellington well enough to catch him, and well enough not to damage him mentally even more than he was already damaged. He tried again.

'Let us say,' he said, 'as an example, that one of us in this room is a carrier of bubonic plague. Let us say he does not know it, that he himself shows no symptoms of bubonic plague. Soon, those of us in contact with the man will begin to sicken and to die. Our deaths will be horrible, and this carrier will have been the direct cause of those deaths. We may fear him, as being deadly. We may pity him, as being himself doomed eventually by the death he carries with him. But if we hate him, if we *blame* him, we do him a terrible injustice. He is sick, he carries within him a sickness, but he *doesn't know it*. And precisely the same is true of Robert Ellington. He is sick. He carries within himself a mental sickness, which is deadly to those with whom he comes in contact. But he doesn't know it. No matter how much we are revolted by the results of his sickness, we cannot in all justice hate him or blame him.'

'I don't hate him,' said one of the police officers. 'I just want to catch him.'

'Yes. Yes, of course. We all do. Very well. Very well, you want to know what he is most probably doing at this moment.'

'Strangling somebody,' said a newsman flippantly.

'That is a regrettable possibility,' Dr Peterby told him. 'But

I think we all know that already, and don't require to be reminded of it.'

The newsman looked properly sheepish. Those near him shifted uncomfortably.

'You have established,' said Dr Peterby, 'that Ellington escaped with the suitcase belonging to the young man he killed on the highway. He therefore is now in possession of clothing more suitable to the outside world than that in which he left here. He may even have stolen money from the same young man. With clothing and money, I would imagine that Ellington would next attempt simply to disappear in the crowd. I would guess that he would make his way as quickly as possible to a large city, such as New York. I would also guess that he would use the same protective device in the outside world which served him so well here. That is, I would imagine that he would attempt to *become* someone else. That he would pick someone he met in a train, perhaps, or a restaurant, study the person's mannerisms and movements and speech patterns and habits of thought, and then mimic that person from then on. He would be attempting to disguise himself as a free man, and I would guess that he would do so by *becoming* one of the free men he meets. Now, his mimicry never lasted long here; he would be a different patient at almost every session. Sometimes, when one of his roles particularly pleased him – he had the most fun, I think, with the patients of lower mentality – he would keep the part for two or three sessions. But normally he would change from session to session, and I would guess he will do much the same thing in the outside world. That each day, perhaps, he will pick out some different person to be. Because of that, and because he will feel himself to be a hunted man, I would imagine that he wouldn't stay in any one place long. I would guess he will live in hotels, changing to a new hotel every day. I would guess he will make no attempt to get a job, afraid of the normal questions asked by any employer, and so, in order to have money for food and shelter, I regret to say that my guess would be he will resort to robbery. He has no background of house-breaking or safe-cracking or anything along those lines, so I would imagine he will be limited to robbery of individuals. What, I believe, is termed mugging.'

'So,' said one of the police officers bitterly, 'we can look for him killing people in Central Park.'

'I'm very much afraid you will find him doing something very like that.'

A newsman said, 'What about the sex angle, Doctor? He's been cooped away here for quite a while. Is he liable to go after women?'

'He has absolutely no history of sexual crime of any sort. Whether or not he will attempt a sexual encounter at this time, I couldn't say. It is possible he will hire a prostitute. It is possible that his fear of exposure will keep him from consciously desiring such intimate relationship with anyone.'

The same newsman asked, 'Is it also possible he may try to get his sex by force, the same way you think he'll get his money? And the same way he got out of here, too.'

'I would not want to see you paint Robert Ellington in your newspaper as a sex maniac,' Dr Peterby told him. 'As I have said, he has absolutely no prior history of sex crime or sexual pathology or sex-based violence. His is a sick mind, a deranged mind. Therefore, no certain predictions can be made about what he will do. It is possible he will attempt rape. It is also possible he will attempt to kill himself. I think both possibilities very unlikely. Remember that while his mind is sick, it is also a highly intelligent mind and a very clever mind. I have no doubt he could carry off a masquerade of normalcy for a limited period of time, with no question in those around him that he is other than what he seems. He is far from inarticulate. He can be, in fact, extremely wordy and facile and chatty, if these happen to be the characteristics of the person he is mimicking. However, and this does relate to the sexual question raised a moment ago, he can be articulate only on non-stress subjects. He cannot express a strong opinion of his own, or a strong emotion of his own, through the play-acting of being someone else. Nor can he successfully simulate strong emotion or strong opinion on the part of the person he is imitating. Once strong emotion is brought into play, he is reduced to a mute condition, necessitated by the need to hide his true self from himself.'

A police officer said, 'Doctor, this business about his being in a big city like New York, and stealing to make a living – how good do you think the odds are?'

'What is the chance that I'm wrong?' Dr Peterby smiled. 'A very good chance,' he said. 'You must remember that we are dealing with a sick mind, and we can never be absolutely sure what that mind will do. It is entirely possible that at this very moment Robert Ellington is on a farm somewhere, the newly hired handyman, doing the chores and minding his own business and causing trouble to no one. I think this unlikely, because he has no rural background, and because despite his derangement he is clever. I am basing my guesses on the belief that he will consider his situation, decide that anonymity is his best chance to avoid recapture, and further decide that anonymity is much more readily found in a large city than in either a small town or a farm area, where strangers are much more noticeable. I am basing my guess that he will rob rather than work on the same assumption that he will consider his primary goal to be anonymity and so will take no chances on a regular job.'

He spread his hands. 'There's really nothing more I can add.'

They thanked him, and promised to keep him informed, and the newsmen asked a few more questions in search of the sensationalism which paid their salaries, and slowly the office emptied.

Once they were gone, Dr Peterby switched off the ceiling light. Thick draperies flanked his windows, dimming the sunlight that brightened the world outside. Now in the afternoon the sun was around on the other side of the building, leaving this side in the shade. Dr Peterby switched on the desk lamp, creating a small circle of warm glowing light around the desk. He sat in the middle of this warm circle, picked up his telephone, and phoned someone to come take all those chairs away.

Mel's room was seven by eleven, with an eight-foot ceiling; six hundred and sixteen cubic feet. The bottom was varnished, the sides were painted pale green, the top was painted off-white. This box contained a bed with white-painted metal head and foot, a small and chunky dresser enamelled black, a small walnut-toned table with a green blotter on it to indicate it was a writing desk, two wooden chairs without arms, a scarred black bedside table with uneven legs, and a black metal wastebasket graced on one side by an enormous rose decal. A small green rectangular rug lay on the floor to the left of the bed. There was a mirror on the closet door, doubling everything.

Without the mirror, there were three light sources: a ceiling fixture shaped vaguely like a flying saucer, a gooseneck lamp on the writing table, a pink-shaded porcelain-bodied lamp on the bedside table. All three were lit. The six-hundred-sixteen-cubic-feet box was bathed in light.

It was 9:15 p.m. Mel lay on the bed, supine, gazing at the ceiling.

The policeman, Sondgard, had finished with the individual interviews a little before seven. Then he'd come in and talked to them all together. He'd thanked them for their cooperation, and then he asked them if they would cooperate with him further. There were only two things he wanted from them: First, if anyone remembered anything that might be of any help at all, he or she should get in touch with Captain Sondgard at once. And second, none of them were to leave Cartier Isle until further notice.

After that, there had been a silent awkward dinner, with all of them only picking and poking at the food. For a while they could hear Captain Sondgard in the hall, talking with the doctor who had examined Cissie Walker, and then an ambulance had come to take Cissie away, and for a while the house was full of the rumbling of men going up and down the stairs.

Mel spent ten or fifteen minutes at the table, but ate practically nothing, and finally gave up and went upstairs. The door to Cissie's room was open, and though he tried to avert his eyes he couldn't help looking in there. She was gone now, of course. The other policeman, the one called Mike, had a little kit laid out on the bed and was dusting all likely places in search of fingerprints. Also, Mel's suitcase was still there, just inside the door, where he had dropped it and forgotten it.

He went to the doorway. 'Excuse me,' he said.

The policeman looked around at him, stolid and impassive.

'That's my suitcase.'

'It is? What's it doing here?'

'I dropped it when I – found her.'

'Oh, yeah, that's right. You're Daniels. Go ahead, take it.'

'Thank you.'

He had taken the suitcase, and then at last he had found the empty room, this room in which he now lay on the bed and stared at the ceiling. Across the hall, the policeman named Mike was or was not still looking for fingerprints; Mel had his own door closed, and didn't know if the policeman had left yet or not. Elsewhere in the house, presumably, the other members of the company were sitting around and waiting, as he was waiting.

They wouldn't be working any more tonight, of that he was sure. Would they work together at all again here this summer? They would all be staying here, at least for a while, but only because they couldn't leave.

If there was no season here, that would mean no Equity membership this fall. It was far too late to get a spot at some other theatre. This whole thing could throw him back a full year.

And then, while he was thinking this, suddenly on the white ceiling, like a colour slide all at once projected there, he saw again Cissie Walker's bedroom this afternoon, and Cissie herself dead on the bed. He shut his eyes, and the colour slide was projected on the inside of his eyelids instead.

The knocking at the door startled him so that he leaped up from the bed. 'Who is it?' He shouted it much louder than necessary.

'Bob,' said the muffled voice. 'Bob Haldemann.'

'Oh. Come in.' Mel started across the room to open the door, but it opened before he got there, and Haldemann came in. Mel said, 'You shook me up a little bit. Knocking on the door there.'

'I'm sorry. I know, we're all nervous here now.'

'Sit down.' Mel went back to sit on the edge of the bed. 'I wish I had a radio in here,' he said. 'A television set would be nice, too, but I'd settle for a radio.'

'Some of the boys have gone over to the Lounge,' Haldemann told him. 'You could go on over there, if you like.'

'I think I will. You going over?'

'No, I can't. There's still work to do. What I wanted to see you about, I imagine we'll be getting reporters tomorrow morning. I'd appreciate it if you wouldn't talk to them, Mel. I'm asking everyone the same thing; if a reporter approaches you, refer him to me. I imagine they'll be flocking around you in particular, since you found the bo – uh, well, found the body, I guess that's the only way – but all I mean is, I wish you'd just refer them to me.'

'Sure.'

'At first glance,' Haldemann said, 'I suppose this – this *thing* here, I suppose it looks like it would be, well, *publicity* for us. As though it would bring us a lot of additional business, from the curious, you know, the people who always flock to a thing like this. But —— You see, the way I look at it, it wouldn't be good publicity at all. This whole affair is sensational enough as it is, and if it looked as though we were trying to capitalize on it, well, we'd attract the curious, of course, the kind of people who come once and then never show up again. But I think we'd drive away the people we need to support us for an entire season, and for next season, and so on. I mean, it's going to be very difficult *not* to look as though we're trying to capitalize on it. An affair like this, you know, it's bound to be given sensational treatment in the newspapers anyway. But I want to, I want to *limit* it as much as I possibly can, and so that's why I don't want anyone to talk to reporters, but just to refer them to me. Because you might have the best intentions in the world, but you never know how what you say is going to look in print, or how they can take things out of context. So, if you'll just do that for me, I'd appreciate it.'

'Then, we will have a season here?'

'Well, I'm not sure. I mean, I hope so, certainly. There's an investment, not only mine but everybody else's, too, and of course there's been a continuity to this theatre, eleven consecutive seasons and we've never so much as missed a performance, but at this point I'm just not sure if it will be possible. We all have to stay anyway, at least for the time being, and I'll want to talk to Eric Sondgard and see what he thinks, and so on, and try to let everyone know one way or the other just as soon as possible.'

Haldemann got to his feet. 'I'll see you later, Mel,' he said. 'And of course you know how much I regret all this.'

'Well, sure.' Mel was surprised again at Haldemann's eternally apologetic manner. Haldemann was always apologizing for something that wasn't his fault and over which he had no control. Like Ralph Schoen. Or the murder. The man just didn't jibe with Mel's preconception of a summer-theatre producer.

Haldemann went out, still murmuring apologies, and Mel was left alone again in his cube. He was fully dressed, but he'd taken his shoes off when he'd come up here after dinner, and now he put them back on again. Anything would be better than solitary confinement in this box, with its unexpected and unwelcome slide projections on the ceiling.

There was an old-fashioned key in the door, on the inside. Mel took it, switched off the light, and locked the door behind him. He noticed that the door to Cissie Walker's room was now closed. All the doors on this floor were closed, in fact, leaving the squarish hallway looking like another box. A magician's box, lined with doors. Or something from one of those labyrinthine Chinese houses in Sax Rohmer.

He went downstairs and outside. The night was clear and cool; the sky velvet-black and sprayed with stars. A thin sliver of moon hung high over the lake.

The house he had just left loomed dark and bulky behind him. A light was on behind one second-storey window, and the downstairs hall light shone through the glass in the front door, but other than that the front of the house was dark. The theatre next door, the night having robbed it of its bright red veneer, was now only a barn again, hulking and silent and dark.

Across the road and down a ways to the left was the only bright spot in the night. A sprawling two-storey stucco building was awash in light. Varicoloured light shone from all its windows. A large and nearly empty parking lot at its side was lit by floodlights. A bright red neon sign in front of the building gleamed out:

BLACK LAKE LOUNGE

Dinner *Dancing*

BAR

Mel turned in that direction, walking along with his hands in his pockets, his shoulders unconsciously hunched to protect the back of his neck from the darkness. He was relieved when he came within the aura of light surrounding the Lounge. Taking his hands from his pockets, he strode across the blacktop and up on to the veranda.

The façade of the Lounge was Southern plantation, complete with pillars and veranda and white front door. But inside the disguise was dropped completely; the interior was the stock bar décor to be found anywhere in the United States. A horseshoe-shaped bar dominated the centre of the room, with booths at the side walls. The normal beer and whisky displays, with all their flashing lights and moving parts, were crowded together on the back bar amid the cash registers and the rows of bottles. Most of the light came from these back-bar displays, aided only slightly by the coloured fluorescent tubes hidden away in the trough that girdled the room high up on the wall. Lithographs of fox-hunting scenes predictably dotted the walls, and the imitation gas lamps jutting from the wall over each booth said *Schiltz* around their bases.

In the rear wall, to either side of the horseshoe bar, were wide arched entranceways leading to the dining-room. In there were all the usual square tables with their white tablecloths and their place settings for four. And off to the right, flanked by maroon draperies, was the broad carpeted stairway to the second floor.

The bar was nearly deserted. Only one bartender was working, and there were no waitresses out here; it was still too early in the season. Two men sat together at the bar, chatting in a desultory manner while they ate cashews and drank beer. A man and a woman – he florid and wealthy-looking, she machined and expensive-looking – sat across from one another at a booth to the left. And finally, four people from the theatre company sat at a booth on the right. They were Tom Burns, the stage manager, whom Mel hadn't met until just before dinner, and three of the actors, Ken Forrest and Will Henley and Rod McGee, the three who were, like himself, all new here this year.

Mel walked over to their table and said, 'Could you use a fifth, or are you all sticking to beer?'

Tom Burns looked up and smiled broadly. 'Well, well, the tattletale! Get yourself a chair. Join us for the post-mortem.'

'Be right with you.'

Mel went over to the bar and got himself a beer. Then, because the booth would only fit four comfortably, he commandeered a chair, and brought it over.

Rod McGee, the thin eager cheerful one, was saying, 'What do you think of that cop anyway? What's his name, Sondgard? What do you think of him?'

'An extremely able man,' Tom Burns started to say, but Will Henley, big and dour, overrode him, saying, 'I don't think much of him. He doesn't know his ass from his elbow, if you ask me.'

'I've known Eric a number of years,' Tom Burns told him, 'and I believe he may surprise you.'

'He's a teacher,' said Ken Forrest. His voice was low, almost diffident.

Mel said, 'A teacher? What kind of teacher?'

'English,' said Tom Burns. 'I don't recall the college at the moment. Isn't it someone's turn to go for refreshments?'

'Yours,' said Henley.

But Rod McGee was already on his feet, saying, 'No, it's mine. Five beers. You ready, Mel?'

'I will be.'

McGee hurried away, and Mel turned to Ken Forrest. 'You mean he isn't a full-time policeman?'

'No, he's a teacher.'

'He works here summertimes,' Burns explained.

'Fine,' said Henley sarcastically. 'A part-time cop. He's an amateur, for God's sake. You really expect him to catch a clever killer?'

Ken Forrest echoed, 'Clever?' His voice was still low, his manner that of a shy man unsure of his acceptance in any group conversation.

Henley slapped him down at once, saying, 'Of course, clever! A lot more clever than our English teacher.'

Forrest retired deeper in his corner, and studied his empty beer glass. It was Mel who picked up the ball for him. 'He doesn't seem so clever to me. He acted like an animal. That doesn't seem clever.'

'Why not? Cunning as a fox, you've heard that before.' Henley's whole tone was belligerent; he leaned far over the table, frowning as he talked. 'Here we've got a house full of people, maybe, I don't know, how many of us? Ten? And this guy comes in and kills somebody right under our noses and goes right back out again and doesn't leave us a hint of who he is or where he came from. You don't call that clever?'

Mel said, 'You think it was somebody from outside, then.'

'I don't know, what difference does it make? One of us, maybe? In that case, he's even *more* clever. He managed to leave us, go commit his murder, and come back, without any of us suspecting what he'd done. Face it, this guy isn't stupid. Now, I don't say this Captain Whatsisname is stupid either, all I say is this killer knows his business and Captain Whatsisname *doesn't* know his business. He may be the greatest English teacher in the world, but as a cop he makes a good English teacher. Thats 'all *I* say.'

Rod McGee came back with the fresh beer then, and the

subject shifted. For a while, they talked about the likelihood of there being a season here this summer. Bob Haldemann had told them all the same thing, that he hoped there would be but he couldn't be sure yet.

They were rather widely split in their opinions. Tom Burns thought there would be a season, but he guessed the opening would be postponed, maybe a week. Will Henley thought, loudly, that there wouldn't be a season, that once this thing was settled most of them would want nothing more but to get away from this part of the country as quick as possible, so there wouldn't be the personnel to put on any plays. Ken Forrest stated with characteristic quiet that he thought the show would go on, but offered no amplification. Rod McGee said he for one was willing to stay if Haldemann decided to go ahead, but he wasn't so sure Haldemann would want to; Haldemann seemed like a pretty sensitive guy, and he might decide it wasn't in good taste to go ahead and put on plays.

Mel had no strong opinion one way or the other yet, so he said nothing. He was, in fact, thinking of something else entirely. For the first time, the idea had become real to him that the killer was very possibly one of the people in the company, maybe even one of the people at this table. He looked at them with this new realization, studying their faces, trying to decide if one of those faces was a mask hiding a murderer.

Tom Burns? The man was obviously a heavy drinker, you could tell from looking at him. He had a careless attitude toward life in general. Could the killing of Cissie Walker have been prompted by alcohol? Had Tom Burns, drunk, tried to force himself on her, been rebuffed, and had he in a drunken rage killed her?

Or Will Henley. He was the biggest and strongest of any of them there; he could most easily have beaten and strangled the girl without giving her a chance to run away or scream for help. And he'd been praising the killer's cleverness; was that simply arrogance? Was he himself the 'clever' killer, mocking them?

Or Ken Forrest. Silent, withdrawn, oddly unemphatic. Couldn't the killer be one of those people who bottles up his emotions, who holds everything in with no safety valve, and who suddenly blows up all at once?

Or Rod McGee. Eager, friendly, agreeable. Another protective cover for a darker person underneath?

The subject of the summer season exhausted, they went on to anecdotes, telling each other half-truths about their past experiences in theatre and the Army and school, and Mel left his morbid reflections alone for a while. He told an exaggerated version of an encounter he'd had with a W A F while touring with an Army Special Services show, and as the talk went on he began to lose the dullness of shock that had been with him since he'd walked into the dead girl's room this afternoon. His normal ebullience returned, and when he managed in the middle of an out-and-out falsehood about a girl guitar player from Queens to let everybody know he was Jewish, he knew wryly he was his old self again.

Gradually, the group was getting more and more animated. They'd all been needing a change of pace, something to break the spell that murder had cast over them, and this was it. From reminiscence they got to the joke-telling period, and not a single clean joke was heard. They were all laughing so hard, and interrupting each other so often, that even the dirty jokes weren't heard any too clearly. In the general hilarity – touched just slightly as it was with hysteria – Will Henley thawed and became absolutely amiable. Ken Forrest came way out of his shell and demonstrated a piercing laugh that endangered every wineglass in the place, and Rod McGee settled in with the group and stopped looking as though any second he would dash off and shine a lot of shoes. As for Tom Burns, his eyes got brighter and brighter, his nose got redder and redder, and his speech got shlurrier and shlurrier.

They finally left the Lounge at one-fifteen, only because the bartender insisted. Tom Burns tried to exit with a quote from Shakespeare, but whether he succeeded or not he alone knew; by now his speech was almost entirely unintelligible.

Will Henley started the singing, as they moved out across the night away from the Lounge. 'On top of Old Smoky,' he shouted, and they all joined in. Mel took upon himself the job of caller, roaring out the lines before they were sung by everyone else, and wishing he could remember that old Stan Freberg parody so he could shout out some of Freberg's lines.

They angled across the road, weaving and singing, all linked together with their arms around each other's shoulders and waists. Lights flicked on in the house bulking ahead of them, and heads appeared in windows, but they ignored it all. They needed release, the one killer and the four unwilling sharers of his drama; what did they care about disapproving heads in lit windows? They were lit themselves, and to hell with everything.

It was Rod McGee who shushed them all when they reached the porch. From loud caterwauling they shifted immediately to comic silence, tiptoeing into the house, giggling, shushing one another, tripping on the stairs. Alden March met them at the second-floor landing, pique on his face and hands on his hips. 'You ought to be ashamed of yourselves,' he told them, in a loud whisper. 'At a time like this.'

They hooted him down, and staggered on by. Mel and Rod and Will had to climb the additional flight to the third floor, where they whispered incoherent good nights to one another. Mel unlocked his door with not too much difficulty, switched on the light, and entered his room. He closed the door, peeled off his clothing, scattered it around the room, switched off the light, and crawled into bed.

Three minutes later, with embarrassed haste, he got up again to relock the door.

The madman lay frightened and exultant in the darkness, squeezing his hands together and smiling from ear to ear. His room was much like Mel Daniels', and like it now was in darkness. The door was closed, but unlocked, for of them all the madman had the least to fear tonight, and a sliver of light outlined the door all the way around.

Of them all he had the least to fear, but he too was afraid, and afraid of the same thing as all the rest. He was afraid of the madman, of himself. Exultant, but also afraid.

100

Exultant, because tonight he had brought it off. The acid test, the *acid* test. Sitting with them all, joining in their conversation, without suspicion. But also afraid, because in his success he had lost himself, and now more than ever before that was dangerous.

It had happened to him other times, when he was fooling Doctor Chax by making believe he was one of the other inmates. Sometimes it had happened that in the making-believe he had lost touch with himself, the true self and the assumed self had become confused together, and for a while he had not been in control. At such times, a tiny portion of himself – he visualized it as crouching low against the floor in a dark corner – only that tiny portion of himself was still aware, could still differentiate between fantasy and reality, while the rest of him was all taken over by the other being. Times when all but that tiny portion of himself actually *believed* he was that other being. It hadn't happened often, and it never lasted long, so he had never been overly concerned about it.

But tonight he was concerned. In the asylum it had not been dangerous, but here it was dangerous indeed. Here he *had* to be in control, at all times. When it had happened tonight, at the table in Black Lake Lounge, the sliver of self that had retained awareness was terrified, afraid that the other being would make a slip, would say the wrong thing and spoil everything.

But it had worked out, with no danger and no trouble, and so the fear was muted by exultance. They had accepted him. They had made no objection to his joining their group, being a part of their conversation and their laughter and their singing.

And he was pleased with himself. When the story-telling time had come, and the joke-telling time, he had done as well as anyone. What matter that it had been automatic, the work of the other being, out of his own control? The point was that he had not only been accepted, he had managed to take advantage of the acceptance and *actively* to become one of them.

And this afternoon, with the teacher/policeman, that too had been good. Could there possibly be any doubt at all in the teacher/policeman's mind that he was precisely what he claimed to be? (Some of the things he'd said had been direct quotes from the dead actor, the one whose place he was taking, just as some of the stories he had told tonight had come from the same source. But the other being – and this was strange – the other being was *not* entirely patterned on the dead actor. It was, for the first time, an amalgam, a combination of people from his past, with the dead actor only one facet. Maybe that was why the being had taken over tonight so readily; it was a more complex creation than any he had done before.)

Thinking of the afternoon's interview with Captain Sondgard, and the night's laughter with the other members of the company, the madman smiled and smiled, nearly bursting out loud into laughter. It was all so *good*!

He couldn't contain himself, he couldn't remain motionless. He got to his feet and paced the room, barefoot and in darkness, rubbing his hands together and nodding his head, mumbling to himself as he did when not quite talking to himself out loud. His body seemed filled with electricity; vitality coursed through him. He was strong, strong, stronger than he'd ever been before.

The room couldn't hold him. He couldn't be confined now, feeling as he did, he couldn't be confined by anything. He prowled around the room, touching the walls in the darkness, brushing his nervous hands over the furniture, his eyes staring into the blackness, his smiling mouth mumbling as he talked to himself.

'They'll never know, they'll never suspect. I can't be held, I can't be questioned. I'm too clever now, I'll never have to do anything again like the old man and the old woman. My powers are too strong now, they're stronger and stronger. Nothing can hold me now, nothing can stop me. I can be free now, I can stay away from Doctor Chax. I can be safe now from the cruelty, I can keep away from all that. I won't ever be caught again, because I'm too strong now. Those who are hateful and vicious will never have the chance to turn on me, because now I will recognize them. And if I have to kill them, if they force me to kill them the way that girl forced me, I can be clever. I didn't know anything before, that's why they caught me. I didn't try to hide or be subtle, I did what had to be done right out in the open. I didn't understand the world then, I didn't understand the way they all band together, the way the evil protect each other. I did what had to be done right out in the open, and the rest of the evil ones took revenge on me, they locked me away and they tried to force their wills on me with the shock treatments, and now that can't happen any more. If I'm forced to it again, if it has to be done, now I know how, now I can keep them from ever finding out it was me. I can be all over the world, I can go anywhere and do anything and they'll never even suspect me. I can get a mask if I want, I can go out at night to do what has to be done. They can't ever find me and they can't ever stop me and they can't ever get even with me again. I'm too strong for them now, I'm too clever for them now.'

None of it came out in articulated words. He thought the words, and his lips moved, and he made small sounds in his throat, but it was all tumbling, too low to be heard outside the room.

He prowled for ten minutes or more, touching the walls and the furniture, smiling in the darkness, telling himself the same things over and over again, and recounting for himself the part he had played in tonight's conversation, and telling himself he hadn't been suspected, and so never would be suspected. He spent ten minutes roaming and muttering, and then the room was just too small to be lived in any more, he could no longer ignore how close together the walls were.

He got dressed again. His movements were unsure, because of the darkness and his excitement, and also because he was still feeling the effects of the beer he had drunk. It had been more than four years since he had had alcohol, and that was probably another reason why the being had been able to take over so readily. Not that he was drunk; but his high spirits were heightened even more by the exhilaration of alcohol.

He didn't turn the room light on at all. When he was dressed, he crept from his room and locked the door after himself. A twenty-five-watt bulb in a wall socket gave the hallway wan lighting. The madman crept downstairs, not wanting to be noticed. It would seem strange to anyone else, that he should want to go out again, past two o'clock in the morning, but he did have to go. He had to walk outside for a while, with nothing but the sky over him. He had to be able to run if he wanted, and to laugh aloud.

The front door was locked. He left it unlocked behind him when he went out, because he didn't have a key. He moved silently off the porch and across the gravel to the road. Then he turned right, away from the Black Lake Lounge, in the direction of town.

As he walked along, the feeling of delight grew and grew in him. Freedom was wonderful! He waved his arms all around, stretching them out away from his body as far as they would go, and his fingertips touched only air. *Nothing* hemmed him in, nothing. He jumped up into the air, he trotted a few steps, he capered, he danced across the road. Sheltered by the night, defended by his cleverness, protected by his strength, he had won his freedom and he had earned his freedom and now he was enjoying his freedom.

No walls! No heavy-handed dour-faced 'nurses'! No locks and bars! No questions! No 'treatments'! No orders, no rules, no restraints.

Freedom!

He laughed aloud, he shouted. He capered down the road, dancing and leaping, filled to overflowing with wild joy, shaking himself like any long-caged creature newly released.

He raised his head and shouted out a song of his own invention:

> No more Doctor Chax!
> No more hurt and pain!
> They'll never get me back,
> They'll never catch me again.
> No more Doctor Chax!
> No more locks and walls!
> They'll never find me now,
> I've got too smart for them now.
> They'll never hunt me down,
> They'll never lock me away,
> They'll never catch me again,

I'm slippery like an eel!
Good-bye, Doctor Chax!
You can't hurt me any more!
You can't make me cry
Or make me crawl and hide!
You can't tell your lies
And try to make me be bad;
You can't find me now,
Way back in your brown little office.
I'm free, I'm free, I'm free,
I can shout and dance and sing;
I can open doors and run around,
And nobody tries to stop me.

But all at once he did stop. Two overlapping images had come into his mind, drawing together a parallel he had not noticed before now. Two overlapping images. The office of Doctor Chax. The kitchen where Captain Sondgard had questioned them all. The images overlapped, like a double-exposed photograph, joining and blending into one image only at the particular spot where in both instances there was movement. In the office of Doctor Chax – whether he called himself Doctor Reed or Doctor Peterby or Doctor Samuelson, in all the offices so much alike – and in the kitchen while Captain Sondgard was asking his questions, in both places there had been a stillness, a heavy unmoving, all except in one place. The turning of the reels, the one reel turning faster than the other, the tape feeding through the maw of the little machine that gobbled one's words. He had recognized the tape recorder when first he'd gone in to see Captain Sondgard – it had given him a bad moment, in fact – but then he'd forgotten it, in the relief of knowing that Captain Sondgard could not see through his disguise.

But now it came back. Doctor Chax existed in stillness, all save the erratic motion of the tape recorder, the two reels never spinning at the same speed. And now Captain Sondgard too existed in stillness, with but the same single exception.

A sign? An omen? A warning?

Must he understand from this that Captain Sondgard was a

danger? Could it be that Captain Sondgard had a direct connexion with Doctor Chax? *Could he be Doctor Chax himself,* in disguise, playing out another of his vicious games, trying to trick and to trap him, knowing all along that he was really Robert Ellington?

He stood in the middle of the road, all his joy and confidence draining away from him. He shook his head back and forth, and moaned in distress, as he had done in front of the house where he had been forced to kill the two old people. Now that it was all over, now that he had been sure he would never have to kill again – he remembered Cissie Walker, but only vaguely, in an unreal and academic manner, and without clear recollection of the details and the reasons, though he instinctively remembered that the reasons had been valid ones – now, now, now that he had thought himself free, was it to start all over again?

He could afford to take no chances. He was not going back there, back to the asylum, he was not going to fall into their clutches again. He could afford to take no chances, he would have to act wherever danger threatened.

This time, this time he must finish Doctor Chax forever. This time, he must kill Doctor Chax and have an end to it.

He stared down the road. Where was he now, Doctor Chax, calling himself Sondgard? In what brown cranny was he hiding, rubbing his hands together in the warm dim glow of the desk lamp, planning his perversities of the morrow?

If only he knew. If only he knew where to find this Captain Sondgard tonight, he could end it right now, be safe once and for all.

Tomorrow. Sometime tomorrow it would have to be. He would have to be sly, careful, cautious. No one must suspect. Somehow, without arousing suspicions anywhere, he would have to find out the location of Captain Sondgard's lair. And then, tomorrow night, he could finish him.

Tomorrow night.

The thought soothed him, but didn't restore his high spirits. Nevertheless, he didn't turn back toward the house, but started walking again along the road in the direction of town. He walked more calmly now, his face sombre, his gaze downward at the road directly in front of him.

And then, out of the corner of his eye, he saw the gate.

He raised his head, and stared at the gate. It was high and wide, and made of iron, with thick vertical bars and rococo iron scrollwork between. A great heavy lock bound the two sides together at the middle, and at either end they were hinged to foot-square brick pillars with concrete caps.

He stared at this gate, and frowned, and gazed this way and that along the road.

He was fenced in.

He hadn't noted it till now, had paid no attention to it. But the road, all along on the left-hand side, was fenced. Tall wire fencing, thousands of metal diamonds linked together to keep him in. And here, at a break in the fence, brick and concrete and iron, and a great heavy lock.

This couldn't be. He growled deep in his throat; his shoulders hunched, and his hands bunched up into fists. He was *free* now, this couldn't be! Damn their eyes, damn their black souls, they never let him alone!

All right. *All right.* He would take the challenge. They would find out now what manner of man they were dealing with. They would find out now what he thought of their petty harassment.

He went over to the gate, and grasped the iron bars. They were cold and rough to the touch, and night-damp. Beyond them, in deeper gloom, a narrow road curved away into trees. All was darkness.

He started to climb. The scrollwork on the gate helped him, and at the top he was very careful because the vertical bars ended in spikes. He raised himself carefully over these, found footing on the highest scrollwork on the other side, and climbed down again to the ground.

So much for their challenge. Did they think an iron gate would stop him? He was *free* now, and powerful in the knowledge of his freedom. Never would he allow them to limit him again.

He turned away from the gate and started down the road. He had gone barely six steps from the gate when a sudden light flashed in his eyes, and a harsh voice cried, 'Stay right where you are, you.'

The shock, the surprise, the blinding light in his eyes, the sudden fear, all combined, and in automatic response he shrank away. The being took over, all at once, and the tiny spark of Robert Ellington crouched low in its dark corner. Let the being take care of this.

But it was not the one he'd expected. It was not the composite character who had taken over earlier tonight, in the Lounge. It was some other being, some darker creation he remembered only vaguely, from long long ago, from the forgotten time before he was ever in the asylum. Beaten down and subdued by the ministrations of Doctor Chax, it had lain undetected all this time at the very core of him. With freedom, it had slowly begun to emerge. The killings he had been forced to commit had strengthened it, and this sudden surprise and shock and blindness had given it the opening it needed.

Only one small spark of self-awareness was left, and that mite struggled to get back into control. This being, this *thing*, it couldn't be a part of Robert Ellington! Mindless, brutal, fetid with its own horrible memories, steaming and stinking, it was nothing that could ever be a part of him, nothing that he could have carried all this time within himself.

Recoiling, unbelieving, not wanting to believe or know or remember, the last crouching bit of self-awareness went down to black.

The flashlight was ahead and to the right. The madman turned that way, and shuffled forward.

The voice behind the flashlight, on a rising inflection, cried out, 'Stay where you are! Keep back! I warn you, I've got a gun!'

The madman leaped. The only shot went high over his back, and then gun and flashlight clattered away to the blacktop, the flashlight going out as it hit.

The blackness was complete now, but the madman didn't have to see. His hands gripped, found cloth, found a naked wrist. A flailing fist was striking at his shoulder, at the side of his head. His hands moved, closed on wrist and arm, moved

108

again, pressed and levered again. There was a dry and muffled snapping sound, and the guard screamed. The madman's clawing hand found the screaming face, closed down on it, snuffing out the scream.

The guard was dead long before he was finished. He broke, he tore, he pounded. In the silence of the night, the sounds were small and moist and heavy.

The madman rose at last to his feet. His hands and forearms were sticky. His face was smeared with stickiness. A strong odour was in his nostrils.

He moved on down the road.

He came at last to a house, broad and sprawling, built at the very edge of the lake. Smooth lawns surrounded it, darkness enclosed it.

The madman moved around the house, hesitating to enter. No real thoughts were moving in his mind now, only impressions. The impression of danger. The impression that the guard had tried to keep him from coming here, so there must be something of value here for him. But strongest of all, the impression of danger.

Danger emanated from the house. It was so broad, so squat. A wide garage stood near it, and then a boathouse built out over the lake. All the structures emanated waves of danger. The madman roamed back and forth, back and forth, all around the house. If he'd met anyone at all on the grounds, he would have killed again, but instinctively he kept outside the house.

The feeling of danger, the meaninglessness of the prowling, the inaction now after the violent action of before, all combined to weaken the creature that was now in control of the madman, to weaken him and make him uneasy. Slowly, reluctantly, he relinquished control, but not as completely as before. He wouldn't be tucked so far away any more, now that he too had had a taste of freedom.

Self-awareness returned to the madman slowly, and vaguely. He was befuddled, unable to think clearly. His memory of the last half-hour was almost non-existent, but he did know that he was covered with blood. Only this one fact was really clear in his mind.

He felt lost, and small, and alone. He stood on the shore, the lake stretching black and flat out ahead of him, the lawns sloping gently upward behind him, the sprawling house and its outbuildings dark humps to his left. He was tiny, he was too small to measure. Naked and exposed here, with the black unbroken flatness of lake and lawn all around him, he felt like an insect, so infinitesimal and fragile that he could break his own bones apart by a careless quick intake of breath. He could turn now and run, running wildly, *stretching* his stubby legs out ahead, flailing his little arms, and run in a dead straight line across the rolling surface of the earth until he died, and the little distance he would cover would be too small to be recorded by the finest and most delicate measuring instruments.

He looked up. Above him, there was nothing. And nothing, and nothing, receding away like a hopeless shout, and dying out in upper emptiness. And far beyond that, so many millions of times his own scrubby height that the number could not be written, were the cold stars, little white lights of pain at the very top of the sky.

He sank to the ground. He was at the very edge, between lawn and lake, where the ground was wet and cold. His fingers scratched meaninglessly at the ground. Tears dribbled down his face, streaking the ribbons of blood on his cheeks. The bleakest of despair washed over him, like fog. His thoughts were vague and troubled, uneasy with black and red movements, half-caught images, uneasy sensations, unclear suggestions. His head rolled back and forth, and tears stained with blood trickled down on to the ground. Regrets and longings filled his troubled brain.

He could no longer believe in his own cleverness and strength and power. He could no longer believe in the inevitability of his success, the permanence of his freedom.

Out of the confusion and the despair there gradually grew a new kind of strength. He would continue, he would live on, but not because he was any longer sure of his eventual triumph. He would live on because that was his role, because this was the part he had to play. Even if defeat seemed certain, he would keep on until the end. Because there was nothing else for him to do.

He would fight no less strongly now. His commitment was as complete as ever. The only change would be that something had been lost within him. Never again would he feel the exultation that had lifted him earlier tonight. Never again would he caper on a night-black road.

He came up again to his feet, tottering, having trouble ordering his body and maintaining his balance. His mind was clearing somewhat, and he was becoming capable of thinking about the immediate future.

There were still things to be done. Sondgard/Chax still loomed ahead of him, but that was far away, tomorrow or later. The immediate problem was to get through the night.

He had to cleanse himself. And he had to return to the house. And he had to cover any tracks he might unwittingly have left behind him, which could lead Sondgard/Chax to his door.

He stepped forward. Fully clothed, he stepped into the lake, wading out till the water was chest-high. Then he bent forward, and dipped his head down into the cold water. He scrubbed his face and hands, and rubbed his hands over his clothing, trying to wash all the blood away. At last, dripping, he came out of the lake again.

His clothes hung heavy to him. His shoes were soggy weights. But his face was cool, his mind clear. He started home.

It was harder to climb the gate this time, in the wet and heavy clothes, but he made it, falling heavily on the other side, hurting his shoulder. He struggled to his feet and walked away along the road, rubbing his shoulder. He walked sombrely now, heavily, with none of his earlier enthusiasm.

The house was still in darkness, except for the hall lights, when he got back to it. He took off his shoes outside and tied the wet laces together, and hung the shoes around his neck. Then he went inside, and carefully locked the door behind him.

He was about to go upstairs when he glanced toward the farther end of the hall, where the kitchen was, and suddenly realized he was very hungry. His appetite was usually not keen, but now a gnawing emptiness had hollowed out his belly, and all at once he was so hungry his hands were shaking.

He moved down the hall and stepped into the dark kitchen. He didn't turn on the large circular fluorescent light in the ceiling, but did switch on the smaller light over the sink. He opened the refrigerator door and found a bottle of milk and a loaf of bread and a jar of raspberry jam. He sat at the kitchen table and made himself a sandwich, and drank the milk.

He ate two sandwiches and drank the entire quart of milk before the gnawing in his belly went away. Then he sat there a while longer, staring at the opposite wall.

This was where Sondgard/Chax had been sitting. He had sat across the way there, answering the questions. The tape recorder with its syzygetic reels had been placed there, to the right.

Bemused, still gazing thoughtfully into the middle distance, he reached out his left hand and picked up the jar of raspberry jam and turned it upside down. The jam oozed out, plopping on to the kitchen table, falling in slow chunks. His right hand groped for the knife he'd been using – he still didn't look at what he was doing – and he used it now to scrape the rest of the jam out of the jar and on to the table.

Then he got to his feet. At the sink, he washed the empty milk bottle, and the dish on which he'd made the sandwiches, and the jar the jam had come in. He left all three on the drainboard, and then turned back to the table.

He started to spread the jam on the table. At first he used the knife, spreading it as though he were spreading jam on bread, but after a minute he put the knife down and used his fingers. His hands pushed and spread the jam, and when he was finished he stood back and looked at it. His clothes were still soggy and shapeless, his shoes hung around his neck, his hands were smeared with jam.

The table now looked like a great open wound, red and scabrous. He looked at it, but didn't seem really to focus on it. His eyes were vague and filmy, as though he were still gazing into the middle distance while thinking of something else.

He pushed his hands into the open wound. His fingers made

meaningless streaks and snarls on it, like finger-painting. He waved his hands through the mess for a few minutes, and then suddenly turned away and stepped purposefully to the sink. He washed the knife, then washed his hands, then washed the faucets where he had touched them and streaked jam on them.

Just before turning out the light, he glanced over again at the table. Why had he done that? He looked at it, and it was meaningless.

He switched off the light, and went upstairs.

Sondgard stood with his back to the wall. The Hunchback of Notre Dame stood in front of him, laughing, holding his curved hands up to let Sondgard know he would strangle him. Sondgard said, 'Why do you do this?' But the Hunchback's answer was drowned out by the sudden pealing of the bells. The Hunchback glared upward, suddenly enraged, crying, 'Those are *my* bells!' The pealing stopped, and Sondgard, puzzled, said, 'I thought you were a deaf-mute.' And again just as the Hunchback answered, the bells began to peal. 'Why, they're calling *me*,' thought Sondgard, surprised that anyone should know he was here, and he sat up, and it was the telephone ringing.

He rubbed his head. 'A dream,' he mumbled. He'd been dreaming, but he couldn't remember what. Something about a stone wall.

The phone took a deep breath, and rang again. It was way out in the living-room, so he had to get out of bed, kick into slippers, and shuffle out of the bedroom. He crossed the living-room and picked up the phone and said, 'Hello?' His voice was fuzzy.

It was Joyce Ravenfield, sounding frightened. 'Eric, can you get down here? Right away.'

'What time is it?'

'Ten after six.'

He closed his eyes, and rubbed his forehead again. He'd

been up till two this morning, listening to the tapes of yesterday's interviews, with no success. 'Where are you?' he asked.

'At the office. No, wait, don't come here. I'm sorry, Eric, I'm a little shaken. Give me a second.'

'Sure.' He was more than willing. He needed a second himself. He dropped down on to the sofa, and tried to think. It was ten after six and Joyce was calling him on the phone.

And sounding completely rattled.

That was wrong. Joyce was never rattled. Joyce was the most efficient woman alive.

If Joyce was rattled –

'What is it?' he asked. He was suddenly wide awake.

'There's been another one,' she said. 'Larry Temple called me.'

Larry was the college student, working here as a patrolman this summer, and taking the night patrol. Sondgard said, 'Another what? Joyce? Another killing, you mean?'

'I'm sorry, Eric, this is so *stupid*.' She seemed on the verge of tears. 'I came all the way down here, I wasted all this time. I just wasn't thinking, I jumped into the car — It must be twenty minutes now.'

'Take it easy, Joyce, take it easy.'

'I'm *trying* to take it easy! Larry called me because he doesn't know your number yet, and he got mine out of the book. And I promised him I'd call you right away, and then instead of that I got all dressed and came down here. I don't know what's the *matter* with me.'

'Another girl, Joyce? For God's sake, tell me.'

'No, not a girl. You know the Lowndes estate? One of the guards there. They found him this morning, and got hold of Larry, and he called me. And then, like an idiot, I – '

'All right, take it easy. Larry's still out there?'

'Yes, I . . . Yes.'

'All right. Call Doc Walsh. And Mike. Tell Mike . . . Tell him he doesn't have to come in yet, but stand by. And call Dave and tell him to stay off that damn boat today and near a phone, just in case.' This last was Dave Rand, the Floridian who operated the police launch here in the summer.

114

'Right, Eric,' she said. 'And . . . Do you want me to call Garrett?'

Sondgard pressed his hand to his forehead. He could feel a splitting headache coming on. The silent phone hissed in his ear, and finally he said, 'Do you think I should?'

'I don't know, Eric. I honestly don't know.'

He shook his head, not knowing either. 'We'll wait,' he said. 'We'll wait and see.'

'All right, Eric. I'll stay here at the office, in case you need me for anything.'

'Fine. Call Larry, tell him I'm on my way.'

'I will.'

Sondgard hung up and pushed himself to his feet. He was awake now, but the headache was coming on stronger and stronger. He padded back across the living-room and into the bathroom, and drank down two aspirin with a glass of water. Then he stripped out of his pyjamas and took a quick cold shower. He had a lean, hard body, had been slender and hard-fleshed all his life, despite his sedentary primary occupation. It was only in the summertime that he got any exercise at all.

Out of the shower in less than three minutes, he hurriedly scrubbed himself dry, padded nude back to the bedroom, and dressed. The four rooms of his flat – living-room, bedroom, bathroom, kitchen – formed the four quarters of a square, with all rooms connecting to the living-room, but none of the other three rooms connected with each other. This awkward arrangement of rooms filled the second floor of a pleasant white clapboard house on East Robin Road, which Sondgard rented from Mrs Flynn, the widow who owned the house and lived on the first floor. The flat's only entrance was up an outside staircase in the back to the kitchen door. Anyone entering the flat had to go first through the kitchen – edging around the table – and then on into the living-room. The bedroom was then to the right, and the bathroom was tucked in the remaining corner, at the rear of the house and next to the kitchen.

The arrangement of rooms, while somewhat awkward, made for a light-filled apartment. Every room – even the bathroom –

had windows in two walls. Light poured in from everywhere, shining on the overstuffed mohair and chipped varnish which had been Mrs Flynn's contribution to the furnishing of the flat, and the few clean simple pieces that had been Sondgard's later additions. There was his leather chair, a deep dark red, with matching footstool. The small chair-side table with built-in humidor and pipe rack, filled with the pipes he only smoked while reading or listening to music. Hanging on the long wall was a painting by a friend of his back at college: a gnarled tree on an ocean cliff, with storm clouds in the background.

Now, so early in the morning, wan light made the front rooms pallid. The house faced west, so living-room and bedroom got no sun till the afternoon. Sondgard finished dressing, wearing the uniform he disliked but which he had long since accepted as a necessary part of the job, and hurried through the kitchen, bright with long rays of morning sunlight, and down the outside wooden stairs, the banister damp with morning dew.

His Volvo was parked in the wide part of the driveway, beside the garage. He took a rag from under the seat and wiped condensation from the windshield, then climbed in and backed the car out to the street. He turned right and drove the two and a half blocks to Broad Avenue, then turned right again.

Broad Avenue was deserted. It was now six-twenty in the morning. The sun was behind him, glistening on the street, casting long shadows of the occasional slender trees along the sidewalks, making it difficult to tell if the two traffic lights he came to were showing red or green. He turned left at Circle South, and headed out around the lake toward the Lowndes estate five miles from town, two miles short of the summer theatre.

Still not six-thirty, and he arrived at the estate entrance, to see the blue-and-white prowl car parked just inside the now-open gates. A black Mercury was parked next to it. Sondgard turned the Volvo in, left it with the other two cars, and walked over to the group beside the road.

There was Larry Temple, looking very young and fragile in his brave blue uniform. And with him were two older, tougher-looking men in dark grey uniforms with badges on their left breasts. Coming closer, Sondgard could see that the badges each

116

had a number, and surrounding the number the legend: *Trans-Continental Protective Agency.*

They saw him coming. One of the private guards stepped forward, saying, 'You're the captain, right?'

'That's right. I'm sorry I didn't get here sooner, but I wasn't notified till twenty minutes ago.'

'Then you made good time. Come on over, and take a look at this.'

It was ugly. Thrown away on the ground was another uniform like the ones worn by the two private guards. But this one was streaked and stained and torn, and inside it were the broken parts of a man.

'Edward Cranshaw,' said the guard. 'That was his name. I notified the home office already.'

'Identification,' Sondgard started, and then he had to stop. He turned away and swallowed, glad he hadn't had time to eat breakfast before coming out here. His mouth was full of a brackish taste, but nothing more solid than that was coming up. After a second, he tried again. 'Identification can't be easy,' he said.

'Yeah, the face, I know. I didn't identify him by the face. Last two fingers of the left hand, see? Gone. Blown off in the war.'

'Oh. Yes, I see.'

Sondgard drifted back away from the body toward the other two men, and the guard trailed along with him, saying, 'At first, I figured it was an animal got him. I don't know what you get around here, maybe mountain lion or bear, I don't know. I figured maybe that's what it was, but it don't look right. No bites. He's pretty broken up, but he hasn't been bit at all, so I figure it must be a man.'

'Yes,' said Sondgard.

'This rape-killing you had out to the theatre yesterday. You figure this connects?'

'I suppose it does. And it was the other way around.'

The guard looked puzzled. 'What was the other way around?'

'Not rape-killing. Killing-rape. He killed her first.'

'Christ on a crutch.' The guard looked back toward the body, shaking his head. 'It didn't figure to be a personal thing,' he said.

'Eddie wasn't from around this neck of the woods at all. Nobody knew him but Frank and me. Oh, yeah, by the way. I'm Harry Downs, and that's Frank Reilly.'

'Eric Sondgard.'

They shook hands all around. Larry Temple said, 'I don't know if I did the right thing, Dr Sondgard.' He wasn't used yet to the new title, still spoke to him as a student speaks to a professor rather than as a patrolman speaks to his captain. 'I didn't know your number, and it isn't in the book, and Miss Ravenfield was the only one I could think of.'

'You did fine, Larry.' Sondgard was thinking he really should get his phone number listed. The company didn't list the numbers of the summer residents, whose phones were only in operation three months of the year, unless the resident paid an additional fee. Sondgard hadn't ever thought the fee was worth it, since everyone who might want to call him already knew his number or could get in touch with him through the office, but now he was no longer sure. He'd talk to Walter Ravenfield, the Mayor, this afternoon; maybe he could get the town to pay the fee for him, as a necessary police expense.

Harry Downs, the talkative guard, was saying, 'Eddie fired off one shot, but I can't tell if he hit the guy or not. There's blood all over the place, but it could all be Eddie's.'

'No one heard the shot?'

'Nope. Frank was in the car most of the night, checking the property on the other side of the road there. That's where we get the most trouble with neckers and kids looking to raise a little hell. They know better than to come in on this side of the road, toward the lake, but they figure anything over on the other side is just left alone all night. So Eddie was on foot, sticking close to the gate here, and Frank was over on the other side in the car, and I was back in the house, asleep.'

'What time did you find him?'

'Frank found him about five-thirty. That right, Frank? Five-thirty?'

'Five-thirty-two,' said Frank. He was lighting a cigarette, cupping the match though there was only the faintest of breezes.

'So the first thing,' said Harry Downs, 'he come on down to the house and got me. We went through the house first, but nobody was around and nothing was taken and no windows or doors had been forced, so then we come back and checked Eddie out, and then Harry took off in the Merc and found your boy there and clued him in.'

'That was five-forty,' said Larry, 'just exactly.' He seemed pleased that he could give an exact time, and slightly embarrassed that the rest of them might think he was putting on. 'I followed the Mercury back here,' he said, 'and saw the body, and then asked to use a phone. I went down to the house and called Miss Ravenfield, and then I came back here and waited. She called on the car radio a little while ago, and said you'd be coming right out.'

'Dr Walsh should be along, too.' Sondgard turned back to the two guards. To Frank, the silent one, he said. 'You didn't see anybody at all during the night? Not out on the road there, or anywhere?'

Frank shook his head. 'Nobody,' he said. 'And I was awake. I don't sleep in a car in the woods. One thing, I thought I heard somebody singing one time. I was stopped, you know, and out of the car, looking around. Heard it way off. Might of been on the road, maybe a car radio.'

'When was this?'

'Somewhere around three o'clock, I guess. I didn't pay much attention. It didn't sound like anything right on the property.'

'Singing.' Sondgard looked over toward the body, then quickly looked away again. He asked, 'Was the gate open or closed when you came back and found him?'

'Closed. Whoever done it climbed over.'

The other guard, Harry, said, 'I checked around outside. No tyre tracks. Nobody pulled off the road along here last night, or it would have showed.'

'He probably walked, then. And he didn't go down to the house?'

'I don't know if he did or not. He didn't get in, that's all I know. Didn't even try.'

'Windows and doors are kept locked.'

'One hundred per cent,' said Harry. 'I check that out every night before I hit the sack.'

Sondgard looked at the gate, glanced over at the body, then down the private road toward the house and the lake. 'He came over the fence. He killed. Then he turned around and went back over the fence again.'

'He was either teed off or crazy,' said Harry. 'You seen what he done to Eddie.'

'Crazy,' said Sondgard, not liking the word but using it because it was handiest.

A telephone rang. Sondgard blinked, and looked around at the woods, for the moment completely baffled.

Harry said, 'Excuse me,' and walked casually over to the Mercury. He opened the door on the driver's side, reached in, and took out from under the dashboard a telephone receiver. 'Downs here,' he said. He listened. 'Check. We'll be right there.' He put the phone away again and looked over at Sondgard. 'You want to come along? That was old man Lowndes himself. He's found something?'

'Of course. Larry, wait here for Dr Walsh. I'll be right back.'

Larry nodded, reluctantly. It was clear he didn't like the idea of their force being divided in half. He was only twenty, a junior, one of Sondgard's 'specials', those few students every year who give the impression they know they don't know everything, want to learn everything, and are willing to believe their teachers know some of the things they want to learn. He had come here expecting to be a traffic cop for the summer, and Sondgard had expected the same thing. Sondgard had given him the night duty because it was normally quieter and simpler than day duty, and also because he thought Larry would take a romantic delight in the job. Neither of them had expected the job to include standing guard over a brutally murdered human being. Larry was holding up far better than Sondgard could have expected. Partially, he supposed, because Harry and Frank were here. Obvious professionals they were, and the boy would surely give anything to keep from seeming young and useless to them.

Sondgard and Harry got into the Mercury, Harry driving, and

120

as they moved on down the road Sondgard pointed at the telephone. 'Some gadget.'

'Direct connexion with the house. It's a walkie-talkie, fancied up. So they can call us if we're out on patrol and something goes wrong. Somebody tries to break in or something.'

'What was it Mr Lowndes found?'

'Some sort of writing, down by the lake.'

'Writing?'

But Harry didn't know any more, and they drove the rest of the way in silence. Harry stopped the car at the end of the road, in front of the garage, and the two men walked around the garage and down toward the lake.

Everett Lowndes was standing down there at the water's edge. A tall spare old man, he was wearing corduroy trousers and a bulky grey knit sweater. His full mane of white hair shone in the sun from across the lake. He started up the slope when he saw them coming.

'Eric Sondgard! Good to see you again.'

'How do you do, Mr Lowndes.'

They shook hands, and Lowndes said, 'The wrong circumstances for a reunion, though. Come along.'

They followed him back down to the water's edge. The lawn petered out a few feet from the lake, and the ground from there on was dark moist soil. Lowndes said, 'You've got to get just the right angle on it to be able to see it at all. It's scratched into the ground. I just happened to see it, coming down here. There. Can you see it?'

Sondgard could see it. Three words, one beneath the other, scrawled repetitiously in the dirt, the letters wavy and uneven, not all of them complete:

> ROBERT
> ROBERT
> ROBERT

'So he did come to the house,' said Sondgard.

'But not inside,' said Lowndes. 'Of that we are quite sure.'

'He leaves notes,' Sondgard said thoughtfully. 'This is the second one.'

'You think it's the same man? The one who killed that girl yesterday?'

'I'm almost sure of it.'

'And you say he's left another note? But this is hardly a note, is it?'

'The first one was a note. In soap, on a mirror. "I'm sorry." '

Harry said, 'You think he's one of these types really wants to get caught? You know, "Stop me before I kill again".'

'Maybe. He isn't sane, that's all I know for sure. So I don't know how to guess at his meanings.'

Lowndes said, "Do you suppose that's his own name?'

'I guess it probably is. The dead man was named Eddie, wasn't he?'

Harry nodded. 'Right.'

Lowndes said, 'And there's no one named Robert in our household.'

Sondgard looked back away from the lake, toward the road. He frowned, trying to think it through. 'He came over the gate,' he said. 'I don't suppose he came over to kill Eddie. He wouldn't even have known Eddie was there. Not without seeing him. And if he'd seen Eddie, then Eddie would have had to see him.'

Harry said, 'And Eddie wouldn't have let him get all the way over the gate. You don't just jump over that thing.'

'That's right. So he climbed over, and started along the road, and that's when Eddie found him. They fought, he killed Eddie, and then he kept on down here. He didn't try to get into the house, or the – What about the garage? The boathouse?'

'We checked them,' said Harry. 'Locked last night, both of them. Still locked this morning.'

'All right. So he came down here, all the way down to the edge of the lake. Then he sat down, I guess, or knelt down. And he wrote that name on the ground. Probably his own name. But, maybe not. Anyway, then he got to his feet and turned around and left.'

Lowndes said, 'You know, this may seem an odd thing to say, with poor Eddie Cranshaw hardly cold, but I think I feel sorry for that man. I could almost see him just now, as you were describing his movements, and he's really a sad and forlorn figure.'

'He's also pretty dangerous,' said Harry.

'I grant that.'

'I know what you mean,' Sondgard told him. 'I've felt the same way about him.' He looked back toward the road again, and saw the blue-and-white patrol car coming toward the house. 'What's this?' He started up the slope, the other two following him.

Sondgard got to the edge of the blacktop just as Larry braked the Ford to a stop. His face was paler than before, his eyes larger. He leaned over to call through the farther window, 'Dr Sondgard! They want you right away.'

'Who? Is Dr Walsh there?'

'Yes, sir, but this is something else. Something else has happened out at the theatre.'

Mel couldn't sleep any more.

Wakefulness came to him, and he opened heavy eyelids and stared blearily at his room, and by the quality of the light he knew it was far too early for him to be awake. It had been way past one o'clock when he'd gotten to sleep last night. If he wanted to be any good to anybody today, he had to get back to sleep.

But it was no good. First, curiosity forced him to open his eyes again, to find out exactly what time it was. Then he had to poke around on the night table to find his watch, and then he was even more awake. His eyes hurt from the daylight, but still his lids had snapped open and didn't seem to want to close again. He found his watch at last, and it was twenty minutes past six.

Five hours sleep. Impossible.

He fell back on the bed with a groan. He *had* to get back to sleep.

But then last night's beer caught up with him, and he had to get up and relieve himself. The floor was icy cold on his bare feet, and the key didn't want to unlock the door, and then the tile floor in the bathroom was even colder. By the time he got back to bed he knew it was hopeless, but still he kept trying.

And then he couldn't get comfortable. He twisted and turned, and mashed the sheet and blanket down under his chin, and curled his knees up, and nothing did any good. The bottom sheet kept bunching into hard ridges beneath his ribs, and the top sheet and blanket were always hanging off the bed to one side or another, and didn't reach up far enough, and pressed down on his toes.

And he was hungry.

He finally had to give up. He pushed the offending sheet and blanket away and sat up. He picked up his watch again and strapped it to his wrist and looked at it, fully believing that he had been awake half an hour or more, trying to get back to sleep, and it was now only six twenty-five. Five minutes.

So he got out of bed. He dressed, and reached for his cigarettes, and put one between his lips. But even before lighting it he got a presentiment of what the taste would be like, and he put it back in the pack. He grabbed a towel and went across the hall to the bathroom and washed his face and hands, and then went back and finished dressing, putting a clean shirt on that immediately started to itch across the shoulder blades.

He went downstairs, intending to go out to the kitchen and make himself a cup of coffee, but by the time he got to the first floor he'd thought better of it. The shape he was in, he shouldn't mess around with stoves and breakable dishes. Maybe the Lounge would be open across the way, or maybe at least there'd be an employee around who could be talked into letting him have a cup of coffee.

He unlocked the front door and went outside to chill damp air and a yellow-orange sun six feet up from the horizon, right at eye level where it could do the most bad. He squinted away from it, and glanced off to the right, and saw three cars parked in front of the theatre. There was the white Continental, which he now knew belonged to Loueen Campbell, who acted for the joy of it and not the money, and the red M.G., which belonged to Bob Haldemann. But the little old dusty Dodge was there too, and that belonged to Mary Ann McKendrick. What the dickens was she doing here this early in the morning?

He decided to go find out.

He stepped down off the porch and crossed the crackling gravel to the theatre. But all the doors were locked. Eight of them, eight glass doors marching along in a row, and he checked them one by one, from this end to that end, and they were all locked.

She left her car here? She went home without it?

That was silly. He knocked on the nearest glass door. Then he kicked it a little bit. And finally he saw one of the inner doors open, and Mary Ann herself peered across the lobby at him. She identified him, and then she came over and stood on the other side of the glass door and called, 'What do you want?' Her voice sounded muffled and far away.

He just looked at her. He didn't know how to answer the question in five or six words, and five or six words is about as long as a conversation can run at a clip with a locked glass door in the way. She waited, and he waited, and finally he boiled it all down to its simplest form, and shouted it through the glass: 'I want a cup of coffee.'

She looked surprised, and shouted, '*I* haven't got any coffee.'

'Listen, would they be' – he turned his head, and pointed toward the Lounge – 'open this time of – ?' It wasn't any good. He gazed unhappily at her through the glass. 'Do we have to shout through this door all the time?'

'There's coffee in the kitchen,' she shouted, and turned away.

'God *damn* it!'

She turned back, surprised again. 'What's the *matter* with you?'

'Listen,' he shouted. 'You don't have to lock the damn – there's no need to – *I* didn't kill her, for Christ's sake!'

'I never said you did!'

'That captain cleared me, I *couldn't* have done it, the timing's wrong.'

'That's wonderful for you,' she said, trying to shout sarcasm. 'But I have work to do.'

'At six o'clock in the morning?'

She came up close to the glass and studied him intently. 'Are you drunk?'

'No! I'm hung over!'

That last about did it. His head split wide open and the sunlight seared in. He screwed his face up and put his hand to his forehead and turned away. 'Never mind,' he muttered, too low for her to hear. 'Just never mind.'

Behind him, there sounded a series of clicks, and she pushed open the door. When he looked back, she was standing in the doorway smiling at him. 'Every time I see you you're hung over,' she told him. 'Are you hung over every day?'

'Except in Lent.'

'You want somebody to make you a cup of coffee, is that it?'

'I didn't know when Mrs Whatsername came to make breakfast, and if I tried it myself right now I'd blow up the house.'

'She isn't coming at all. She called last night. The killing scared her away. She'll be back when the fiend is caught, and not before. That was her word, fiend.'

'It's as good as any.'

'That's right, you saw her. So I suppose it's all right for you to be hung over again today.'

'Thank you.' He started to reach for a cigarette, then changed his mind again. Coffee first. Then another thought occurred to him. 'Are you *really* working at six o'clock in the morning?'

'It isn't six o'clock, it's after six-thirty. And yes, I really am. Or I was, until you showed up.'

'Do you *always* work at six o'clock in the morning?'

'Six-thirty. And no, I don't. But there is a lot to do, and I don't think I'll get much chance to work later on today.' She smiled and patted his arm. 'Come on, I'll make you that coffee.'

They headed back for the house and he said, 'What do you do here, anyway? I mean, I know what you *do*, publicity and assistant director and all that, but how come? You want to be an actress?'

126

'No, sillier than that.' She seemed less her practical self all at once, younger and more shy.

When she didn't go on, he prodded her, saying, 'Such as what?'

'Director.' She said it so softly, so hesitantly, that he could hardly hear the word; but once it was out, she strengthened, and the words came out of her in a sudden rush. 'I want to be a director, Mel. I know, women aren't even supposed to *think* that way, but that's what I want. I have so many *ideas*, things I want to do – I have playbooks home, hundreds of them, full of staging directions, blocked down to every turn, every step. I have cast lists – you wouldn't believe some of my casting, some of the plays and people I'd like to bring together. And movies!'

They were standing now on the porch, but they weren't getting any closer to the kitchen. She stood there in front of the door, her face animated, her words quick and jumbled, her hands gesturing every which way as she talked. 'There are so many things that haven't even been *tried!* I go to a movie, and I look at a scene, and I say to myself, why didn't they do it *this* way, why didn't they put the camera *here* or *here*, why didn't they get a set that, that – Oh, I don't know, it's just, just – I *see* it all so different! And when I watch Ralph work – he's an awfully good director, Mel, he really is, but I watch him, and I think, why not have the actors do *this* or *this*, why not – You know who's my ideal? Margo Jones, that's who. To have my own theatre, my *own* theatre, and direct, find new plays, and new ways to do them, new, new – new *approaches*. I have it all in my head, and I'm learning more every day, and I don't care what I do, I'll do publicity or get coffee or hold the prompt book, I don't care, just so I – just to be *near* it and keep on learning. Do you see?'

It was too early in the day for Mel to see much of anything clearly, but he did understand the intensity in her, and he reacted to it as he always reacted to selfless intensity, with a desire to be helpful and a feeling of sadness, because this kind of flame so rarely survived for very long, in a world that had no real use for such warmth. His voice was more serious – and

127

compassionate – than he'd expected, as he said, 'Then you ought to be in New York. You won't get anywhere here.'

'Margo Jones didn't work in New York, she worked in Dallas.'

'She worked in New York sometimes, and Cartier Isle is no Dallas.'

All at once, she slumped, as though already tasting defeat. 'I know,' she said. 'But I'm a coward. I'm twenty-two; if I'm ever going to get started it's got to be now. But you can't imagine how New York scares me, Mel. Here, I can make believe I'm still learning, still storing up knowledge, still getting ready for the big day. But to go to New York – I wouldn't know anybody, I wouldn't know where to start or what to do. If I wanted to be an actress, I could start out with little parts, I suppose, and build up. But there aren't any minor roles for directors, there just aren't.'

'Have you ever directed anything?'

'Oh, nothing, nothing.' She shook her head in irritation. 'Just high school, and little shows at church, and sometimes I've taken over scenes for Ralph here, that's all.'

'Well, you've met people here, people from New York. Can't you make any contacts here, people who could help you when you got to New York, or introduce you to somebody else who could help you?'

'I don't know, I suppose – ' She shook her head. 'I'm just a coward, that's all. I don't know if I'll ever go or not. Maybe I'll just start the Cartier Isle Little Theatre for the winter season, and keep on doing publicity here in the summer, and die as the seventy-three-year-old town kook. Come on, I'll make you some coffee.' She pushed open the door, and started down the hallway toward the kitchen.

He followed her, saying, 'Listen, why not go to – ?'

'No, don't. I don't want to talk about it any more. Not right now.'

'Later on.'

'All right, later on.'

They pushed open the swing door and went into the kitchen, and both of them saw it at the same time.

The kitchen table. Covered with red pulp, with an obscene red mass of lumpy sticky pulp, as though raw meat had been chopped up into tiny bits, and blood poured over it, and the whole mess had half coagulated, had started to scab over.

And scrawled through it, wavy jerky lines, narrow lines showing the table top beneath, the lines reading:

BOBBY DID IT

Mary Ann was backed against the wall, staring at it wide-eyed, the back of her hand pressed to her mouth. Her voice threadbare and frightened, she said, 'You'd better call the police, Mel. You'd better hurry and call the police.'

BOBBY DID IT

Sondgard sat in a kitchen chair, his arms folded across his chest, and studied the message with frustration and irritation. First R O B E R T R O B E R T R O B E R T and now B O B B Y D I D I T. And before both of them I ' M S O R R Y.

'He wants to be caught,' Sondgard murmured to himself. That was the maddening part of it. This poor creature, this pitiful and infuriating monster, wanted to be caught. He wanted to be stopped, he wanted to be punished, he wanted to be put away where he couldn't cause any more harm. He couldn't bring himself to just walk up to the nearest policeman and give himself up, so he did the next best thing. He left messages. He let the world know that he was sorry for what he was doing, that he didn't want to do it, that he wanted to be stopped from doing it again, and then he let the world know who he was. Robert. Bobby.

There was only one Robert connected with the summer theatre, and that was its producer, Robert Haldemann. But Haldemann was always called Bob, never either Robert or Bobby. Haldemann, Sondgard was sure, *thought* of himself as Bob, not as either Robert of Bobby.

Besides, Haldemann *couldn't* have done it. At least, the first one he couldn't have done, the killing of Cissie Walker. His time was accounted for, he was not even remotely a suspect.

He wants to be caught, Sondgard told himself over and over again. He wants to be caught. He is leaving us clues, he is trying to let us know. But we are too stupid to understand.

He had let them know quite a bit, be sure of quite a bit. They could be sure now that the same person had killed both Cissie Walker and Eddie Cranshaw. They could be sure that this unknown person was one of the people living in this house. After leaving his name in the dirt near the Lowndes house, he had come back here and left another note, so there could be no mistake. He was here, he was the killer of them both, and his name was Bobby.

Or at least, the name Bobby could be connected to him somehow, could lead to him in one way or another. Because his name couldn't really *be* Bobby. Sondgard had a small tight list of suspects, and none of them was named Bobby.

He went over the list in his mind. The names were four:

> Tom Burns
> Ken Forrest
> Will Henley
> Rod McGee

Tom Burns? There was Bobby Burns, the Scot poet. Was the first name supposed to lead to the last name, and then around to another Burns with a different first name? It seemed complicated and roundabout, but would an insane mind work that way? Sondgard couldn't tell.

All right, what about the rest? Ken Forrest. No connexion there with the name Robert or the name Bobby. Not even a similarity of capital letters. Nor was there any famous person with the name Robert Forrest. The same with Will Henley, no similarity of capital letters, no Robert Henley a familiar name. And Rod McGee? McGee had said his first name was a nickname from Fredric, but could it actually be short for Robert? There was, in any case, a similarity of the capital R in both first names.

Sondgard shook his head in angry irritation. It was worse than a double crostic. Worse than *Finnegans Wake* without a pony. Worse than the detective books so many of his fellow professors – but not his fellow captains – insisted on writing every summer, in which the final clue always came from the author's specialty; an inverted signature in a first-edition Gutenberg *De civitate Dei*, the misspelling of the Kurd word for bird, the inscription on a Ming Dynasty vase, or the odd mineral traces found embedded in the handle of the kris.

Bobby. Bobby. It was a name, or a nickname. It was also slang for British policemen. And a bobby-soxer used to mean a teenager. The word 'bob' in Damon Runyon argot was a synonym for 'dollar'. But so what? None of the suspects was a policeman, British or otherwise. None of them were teenagers. None had a name that was a synonym for 'dollar'.

No, this wasn't going to be a word game. The Bobby scrawled on that table was a *name*, and reinforced by the name Robert in the earlier message. The killer was leaving a direct clue to himself, in twice giving them his name. Somehow or other, it had to be possible to connect the name and the killer togther.

Could he be dealing with one of these split-personality cases? Like *The Three Faces of Eve*, where the different personalities operated completely independent of one another, and even took on different names. Could one of these four people be split that way, have a different personality which every once in a while assumed control, and which was a homicidal personality, and which had taken for itself the name Robert or Bobby?

If so, it was a dead end. There was absolutely no way to guess which of these four people harboured within himself a second personality. If there was complete separation between the two, the 'normal' personality would have no real memory of what the second personality had done, might only know he had a memory lapse at the times the killings took place. He might not even realize that much. The killer himself, waiting with the others again in the rehearsal room, might have no suspicion that *he* was the one being hunted.

Sondgard remembered thinking, when he'd seen that first note scribbled on the bathroom mirror, that he was dealing with a

Jekyll and Hyde, a man whose mind had been confused, and in which confusion the Hyde – the evil part of himself – had been allowed to gain dominance. And now he wondered if it wasn't *actually* a Jekyll-Hyde situation, two distinct personalities operating within the same body.

But how to find Hyde, if Jekyll didn't even know he existed?

Yesterday, of course, as part of normal procedure, he had requested police checks on nearly everyone at the theatre. If Hyde had been acting up before all this, some police organization somewhere might have run across Jekyll before. But it could be that Hyde had just emerged very recently, and had no prior activities. Or, since all of his suspects had lived the last few years in New York City, Hyde might have emerged there and not yet been tracked down by the New York police. The city was so large, and the crime rate so enormous, that there were inevitably great numbers of crimes unsolved. Hyde could have been active in New York without the Jekyll part having yet come to the attention of the police.

All of his suspects had told him they had had no prior trouble with the law, and Sondgard was willing to accept the statements. They were too easily checked. If the Jekyll personality *had* been involved in any other case, even only in the capacity of witness, he would have said so, and he would have had a story prepared. To lie about it, when the truth was so easily obtained, would only be to direct suspicion at himself.

Which implied a Jekyll who knew about the existence and activities of Hyde, which wasn't necessarily true. But if Jekyll *didn't* know about Hyde, he wouldn't have any reason to lie because he wouldn't know there was anything to cover.

Besides, he thought gloomily, it didn't necessarily have to be a Jekyll-Hyde situation at all. There could very easily be only one personality involved: the killer. Able to present a blameless face to the world, and then to turn around and commit the most brutal murders.

The thing to do was find out whether any of the four had ever had psychiatric treatment. He could put a request through to the police departments in their home towns, and also again to the New York City police department. With Will Henley, that kind of checking might be difficult; Henley was an Army brat, brought up here and there around the world. Well, if he'd had mental disturbances, his father would most likely have brought him to an Army psychiatrist, so Sondgard would send a request for information to the Army, too.

But all these things would take time, time, time. And the killer wasn't giving them time. He wasn't one of the old-fashioned slow-working homicidal maniacs who only killed once a month, when the moon was full or his wife had completed a menstrual cycle; this particular maniac had killed twice in two days. And, except for the brutality in both cases, the killings were not at all similar. One was a sex slaying, and the girl was strangled, and it took place in daylight. And the other was the killing of a middle-aged man, and he'd been torn to pieces, and it took place at night. In the first, sex had been the motive; but in the second, there wasn't really any motive at all.

'If we could find out *why* he climbed over that gate,' Sondgard muttered to himself, 'we might have him. He had to have a reason, no matter how crazy or unreal it was. He had to have a reason, and if we can only figure out what that reason was, we'd – '

He was talking to himself.

He said, 'Gahhh!' and rose abruptly from the chair. Talking to himself. He had to finish this thing pretty soon, or they'd be carrying him off instead of the killer.

Talking to himself. Next, he'd be cutting out paper dolls.

Paper dolls. What if – ?

Not paper dolls necessarily. But *something*. Maybe there'd be something, left behind by Hyde.

He made his decision, and strode out of the kitchen. Larry Temple and Mike Tompkins were both standing in the hallway, Larry looking pale and dazed, from a combination of his experiences of the morning and a lack of sleep, and Mike still looking sheepish because of yesterday's fingerprint fiasco.

They had been *that* close. One fingerprint away, and Mike had blown it.

The thing was, the killer had made absolutely no attempt to avoid leaving fingerprints. He hadn't worn gloves, and he

133

hadn't wiped any surfaces clean before leaving. That was probably another indication of his desire to be caught and stopped. But he'd been excited, nervous, tense, while killing Cissie Walker, and his fingers had been trembling. Smudged prints were everywhere, and none of them useful. Only one print had seemed like a good possibility; a right-thumb print smashed into the bar of soap the killer had used to write on the mirror. The soap was pale green, and Mike had dusted it lightly with the black powder, bringing out the highlights of the print and seeing that it was probably a pretty good one, though they couldn't be sure until the photo was enlarged. But then he'd set the bar of soap up to take the picture, and the soap had slipped away as soap will do, and unthinkingly he had lunged for it and grabbed.

It could have happened to anyone. Sondgard had told him so, and had meant it – though he couldn't entirely hide his disappointment – but Mike hadn't been able to accept the solace. 'Would one of Garrett's men have loused it up like that?' he'd asked.

No, probably not. Sondgard had had nothing to say.

Because if one of Garrett's men wouldn't have loused it up, like that, then Mike should no longer feel responsible or take the blame on his own shoulders. It was Sondgard's responsibility, the blame rested squarely on *his* shoulders, because it had been his decision not to call Garrett in.

If he'd called Garrett right away, yesterday, as soon as he'd learned the seriousness of the crime, would Garrett have cleaned it up by last night? Would Eddie Cranshaw still be alive?

No, not with the evidence so far. Not even Sherlock Holmes could have found the right man that quickly, and been *sure* enough to make an arrest.

Except that Garrett would probably have had the print.

If the print had been usable. It could just as readily have been no good at all, like every other print Mike had found. Mike had taken pictures of five different prints, and when enlarged none of them had been worth a damn. So maybe the thumb print on the bar of soap wouldn't have been worth a damn either. But there was no way to know that for sure, one way or the other, so Mike was still looking sheepish this morning, and Sondgard would never know whether he had been to blame for Cranshaw's death or not.

They had to get him. They had to get him soon, before he piled any more crimes on Sondgard's conscience.

What about Garrett now? Why not call him in? In a way, Sondgard would welcome it, would be more than happy to have Garrett relieve him of the responsibility, but in another way he couldn't do it. Pride was part of it, he had to admit that, and embarrassment at calling Garrett in so late to repair the botched job, but there was also Sondgard's own stubbornness and his conviction that he was still better qualified than Garrett to catch this particular killer, because this particular killer was not going to be caught by fingerprints or lab work, this particular killer was going to be caught only by an understanding of human nature.

It was Sondgard's baby, and he was stuck with it.

He came down the hall and said, 'Anything out of them?'

Mike shook his head. 'Not a peep.'

'They haven't been told about Cranshaw, have they?'

'Nope. They still think it's just that kitchen-table deal.'

'All right. Good. I'll be right back.'

Sondgard slid open the door and stepped into the rehearsal room, closing the door again behind himself. Fifteen people sat on the folding chairs, their heads turned to look at him, their faces curious and troubled. Eleven men and four women. One of four of the men was the killer. Any one of the others could be his next victim.

Sondgard moved up to the front of the room, by the sofa and table, where under normal circumstances these people would be rehearsing their first week's play right now. Well, maybe not right now; it was barely eight o'clock in the morning. Many of the faces out in front of him showed the marks of too-little sleep and too-rude an awakening. And none of these people had had breakfast yet, or so much as a cup of coffee.

Sondgard had arrived at the house with Larry Temple, having called Joyce to get in touch with Dave Rand and have him take over on the scene of the second murder. Doc Walsh was already there, and the ambulance would be arriving soon, and so would the state technical people. These last were a different proposition from Captain Garrett; since the town hardly had a crime lab of its own, state personnel and state facilities were automatically used for this facet of any local criminal investigation, whereas Captain Garrett of the state C.I.D. office couldn't come in on the case unless requested by Sondgard. (It was unfortunate, Sondgard reflected, that the state technical assistance didn't extend to the taking of fingerprints, but even a town the size of Cartier Isle could afford the powders and camera, and Mike Tompkins had received training in taking prints at the State Police Academy.)

At any rate, he and Larry Temple had come here direct from the Lowndes estate, both in the patrol car, leaving Sondgard's Volvo back by the gate where the murder had taken place. Sondgard had seen the mess on the kitchen table, had questioned Mel Daniels and Mary Ann, got both their stories, and then had them rouse everybody else out of bed. They were all given time to wash and dress, and then they were assembled in the rehearsal room. They all knew about what was on the kitchen table, but none of them – except the killer – knew about the murder of Eddie Cranshaw.

Sondgard had made them wait in the rehearsal room, while he sat gazing gloomily at the kitchen table, not so much as a bit of tactical psychology but because he hadn't been sure exactly what he would say to them or what he would ask of them. But now that they were in front of him, half-ideas and embryonic schemes were suddenly filling his head.

But one thing at a time. He began by saying, 'You all know what's happened. Someone last night smeared jam on the kitchen table and then wrote, "Bobby did it", in the mess he'd made. We can only assume that what was meant was that somebody named Bobby is the one who killed Cissie Walker. We're also assuming that the same person was the one who left us that message. Are we wrong about that? Did the same person kill Cissie Walker and then leave us that message? Or is there someone here who knows who the killer is, or thinks he has evidence to prove who the killer is, and who left us that message because he or she is afraid to make an open accusation? If so, if whoever you are who left that message you are *not* the same person who killed Cissie Walker, you haven't helped us. In fact, you've only served to confuse us. So I'll ask you to come forward and straighten out the confusion. And if you'd rather not get up in front of everybody, I'll be around here the rest of the day and you can come to me at any time.'

Only silence answered him, and an uneasy rustling and shuffling of feet. Sondgard took a deep breath, and went on to step number two. 'In the meantime,' he said, 'we've decided it's necessary to make a thorough search of this house. That means, of course, a search of your rooms as well, and your possessions. If necessary, I can go to a judge and get a search warrant, but that would take time I'd rather not spend. I'd like your permission instead. Does anyone object to his room and possessions being searched? I promise you nothing will be disarranged, and certainly nothing will be stolen.'

Again, only silence.

'Then I have your permission, is that right? No one objects?'

Faces were turning, they were looking at one another, waiting to see if anyone would object, because who would object other than the killer? But no one spoke.

'All right,' said Sondgard. 'Now, there's one more point.' He hesitated, because what he was planning now was dangerous, could backfire badly if it didn't work. And he hadn't had time to think it out beforehand, since it hadn't occurred to him until he was standing right here in front of these people.

Well, it was sink or swim.

'There's one more point,' he said again. 'We have what we believe is one good fingerprint. It's a right-thumb print, and we got it from the cake of soap the killer used when he wrote, "I'm sorry", on the mirror. We've photographed the print and sent it down to the state capital for enlargement and copying. At the time, we still couldn't be sure whether Cissie Walker's killer was someone living in this house or not, so we asked that the thumb print simply be run through the normal check in the F.B.I. files in Washington. But now, because of what happened last night, there's no longer any doubt. So I've called the state police at the capital, and I've asked their assistance. They will be here at three o'clock this afternoon, with equipment and personnel to take the fingerprints of everyone living in this house. All we'll have to do after that is match our thumb print against the prints we take this afternoon. I believe, therefore, that I can assure you that this whole business will be over by this afternoon, but between now and then none of you are to leave this building without my express permission.'

He paused, thinking over what he'd said, and preparing what he was to say next. The obvious flaw in his little lie was the fact that he intended to search the house. If they had such a great clue, and it was going to give them the killer at three o'clock this afternoon anyway, why bother to make the search? It was a question that might occur to the killer, and it had to be answered now. Also, in case this didn't work out, it would be nice if Sondgard had left himself an out. So he proceeded to kill two birds with one stone:

'I told you that I *believe* this whole business will be finished this afternoon. But we can't as yet be sure. I don't know if any of you know much about fingerprints and their detection, but they are far less useful and far less frequent than detective stories might lead you to believe. The killer, as a matter of fact, left prints all over Cissie Walker's room, but they were all smeared and smudged and useless, all except this one print on the cake of soap. Now, that looks like a good print to the naked eye. And it looks like a good print in a small negative. And it looks like a good print in a contact print from that negative. But we won't really be able to tell if it's a good print or not until we get the answer from downstate, until after the enlargement has been made. I would say right now that the chances are ninety-ten that it is a good print, and that we won't need any more. But there is, I must admit, that one chance in ten that it *won't* be a good print. Just in case, I intend to go ahead as though we had no print at all. We are dealing with a madman, and I don't want to waste time, I don't want to sit around an entire day waiting for one clue, if there's even the remotest chance that the clue won't turn out as good as we'd expected.'

Again he paused, and again he looked over what he had said. It sounded good to him, and he was a little surprised at his ability to lie extemporaneously. Maybe he'd chosen the wrong professions, maybe he should have been a lawyer. Or a politician; he could do television debates with the best of them.

He was pleased with his lie. It had a fullness to it. It was so full with details and facts, so ringed around with secondary truths, that he couldn't see how anyone could challenge the primary lie.

It should work.

If it worked, someone would make a run for it before three o'clock this afternoon.

If it didn't work, Sondgard had no idea what he'd try next.

Then he remembered *The Three Faces of Eve* again, his Jekyll and Hyde theory. What if Jekyll were in control right now, and he was standing up here threatening Hyde? Jekyll might not even know there was any *reason* to make a run for it.

But didn't Eve's secondary personalities have contact with the primary personality? As he remembered it, the primary personality knew nothing about the second and third faces, but they *did* have knowledge of her, and did have some awareness while she was in control.

It didn't matter. Maybe the killer was a Jekyll and Hyde, and maybe he wasn't. Maybe he knew what was going on, and maybe he didn't. But at the moment it just didn't matter; Sondgard had already committed himself.

He said, 'That's all for the moment. Now, I imagine you all want your breakfasts. Mrs Kenyon won't be working here for a while, and I don't suppose any of us can blame her, so you'll have to root for yourself. We've already got our photos of the kitchen table, and we've finished with everything else in there, so you can have it back. I suggest the girls go out now and rustle up some breakfast for everyone. If you have extra, I could use some food myself.'

Mary Ann McKendrick spoke up, the first to break the general silence of his audience: 'Is it all right for us to clean the table?'

'Yes. Go ahead.'

Tom Burns was next. 'What about us boys? You want us to stay in here?'

'For just a few minutes, yes. I'll have a few questions to ask some of you, individually.'

Sondgard stood at the front of the room a moment longer, though there was nothing else to say, and as long as he remained there no one else moved. Then he turned and walked toward the door, breaking the spell, and the four women got to their feet and trailed out of the room after him. They headed down the hall toward the kitchen, and Sondgard went over to Mike, who had motioned to him. 'What is it?'

'There's a wire-service stringer outside. Transworld Press. What do we do?'

'Tell him to wait a minute.' Sondgard went back, slid open the door again, and called into the low buzzing that had filled the room once he'd left it, 'Bob, could you come here a minute?'

Haldemann got to his feet and came hurriedly across the room. He stepped out to the hall, and Sondgard slid the door shut again, saying, 'Bob, our first reporter's out front. You want to talk to him?'

'If it's all right, yes.'

'It's all right. But I don't want anyone else in the company talking to him, or any other reporter.'

'I've already told them that.'

'Good. Another thing, I don't want him told anything about what we've got in the works. The fingerprint, or searching the house, or anything like that. You can tell him all about the murder, and the names of the people in the company, and anything else along that line, but the investigation is private.'

'Of course, Eric. Anything you say.'

'Fine. I suppose he'll have to have a statement from me, so I'll go talk to him now, and then you can have him. Oh, by the way. Our belief that the killer is necessarily someone in the company is also private. As far as the press is concerned, the killer could be someone in the company, or someone in town, or someone who just passed through.'

Haldemann nodded. His expression was serious and worried; Sondgard had no doubt he would strain himself to do the right thing.

Sondgard left him in the hallway and went out on the porch

to talk to the reporter, a burly red-haired man carrying a small sleek camera. 'Shots of the buildings and grounds are all right,' Sondgard told him without preamble. 'But shots of the people involved are out.'

The reporter seemed taken aback. He'd clearly expected a more gentle tone, or at least a hello to start things off. He said, 'How come?'

'Because the investigation is still in progress, and I don't want you in contact with any of these people but the producer, who'll be out to talk to you in a minute.'

The man shrugged. 'I'm not pushy, mister,' he said. 'I'll take whatever you give me, and thank you.'

'All right, fine.' Sondgard felt himself relaxing somewhat. He'd made himself far too nervous and tense with that little bluff he'd tried in there, and so he'd been more brusque than he'd intended with the reporter. He said, 'I really don't mean to chew your head off. It's just that this thing isn't over yet, and I don't want more elements in it than I can control.'

'Do you have any leads?'

'Of course. We're working on them.'

'But nothing for publication.'

'Not yet.'

'Could I have your name ,sir?'

'Eric Sondgard. Captain Eric Sondgard, Cartier Isle Police Department.'

'I understand this is only your summer work, Captain, you're a college teacher the rest of the year. Is that right?'

'That's right. But I really don't have time to be interviewed right now. I came out here mainly to ask you what may seem like a very strange question, but I'd like you to answer it anyway.'

'I'll do my best.'

'Fine. Just what are you here to report on?'

The reporter frowned. 'How's that again?'

'What case am I working on?'

'Well – The murders.'

'Murders?'

'Yeah, the . . . ' The reporter was now at a total loss. 'The killing of the actress yesterday, and that private eye that got killed last night.'

Which was what Sondgard wanted to know; the red-haired man had already heard about the second killing. He said, 'As a part of the investigation. I've kept the information about that second killing from the people inside, including the man who'll talk to you. I don't want you to mention it to him. Talk to him exclusively about the first murder. Understand?'

'No,' said the reporter, 'but I'll do it.'

'Fine. When you finish talking with him, let me know, and you can talk to Officer Temple, the first policeman on the scene at the second killing. He can give you all the information you want on that one.'

'Fair enough.'

'All right, good.'

Sondgard turned away, but the reporter called to him, and when he turned around again, said, 'I'm the first reporter here, right?'

'Yes, you are.'

'I can do you a favour, Captain Sondgard, if you'll do me one.'

'Such as?'

'Make me press liaison. I'll get the facts from the people you let me talk to, and any other reporters who show up can talk to me. I'll keep them from getting in your hair.'

'That would be fine. What's the favour I do in return?'

'Give me first word when you get him.'

'I'm not sure that would be so easy to do.'

'Easiest thing in the world, if I'm press liaison. Just allow me to sit on the information ten minutes. That's all I need to get my call in, and have Transworld first with it on the wire.'

'Is that legal?'

'Sure. It's only unethical, but it's legal. And how's it going to get back to you? *I'm* the one sits on the information. You gave it to me to pass on, and I held it ten minutes. All I ask is you don't notice how long I take to spread the word. Okay?'

Sondgard thought it over. It was certainly fair, a favour for a favour. And this red-haired man *was* the first reporter to arrive.

And it would be a relief to know someone else was handling the reporter angle.

He nodded. 'Okay,' he said. 'And, what's your name?'

'Oh, didn't your officer tell you? I gave him my card. It's Harry Edwards.'

'Harry Edwards. All right, fine. The producer's name is Bob Haldemann. He'll be out in just a second. You can talk with him in his office over at the theatre.'

'Thanks.'

Sondgard stepped back inside, and said to Haldemann, 'He's all yours. Name's Harry Edwards.'

'Right. Oh, Eric, about that thing in the kitchen – "Bobby did it" – do I talk about that?'

'Yes, I think so. A simple description of the facts, and that's it. Oh, that reminds me, something I forgot. I'll go back out with you.'

The two men went out on to the porch, and Sondgard performed the introductions, then said, 'The reason you're talking to Bob is because he's one of the people we've completely eliminated from suspicion. His time is totally accounted for.'

'Glad to hear it,' said Edwards. He grinned. 'I don't know as how I'd feel right, going into that empty theatre with one of your live suspects.'

'You have no worries.'

Sondgard went back inside. 'Larry, come here a second.'

Temple came over, looking more and more pale and bushed.

Sondgard said, 'I'd like you to stick around just a little longer. When the reporter's done with Bob Haldemann, he'll want to talk to you about the second killing. Give him any facts he wants to know, but nothing about the investigation, right?'

'Sure, Dr Sondgard.'

'You'd better sit down some place till he's ready for you. You look ready to drop.'

'I'm okay.'

'I know you are. Mike, come on along with me.'

'Where we going?'

'To search the rooms. We're going to take this place apart, piece by piece.'

'What are we looking for?'

'I don't know. What would a madman have in his room? Paper dolls he's cut out? A Napoleon hat? Maybe he writes notes to himself, too.'

'All right, we can try it.'

'That's what I thought.'

Sondgard took two steps up the stairs, and then said, 'Oh, damn! I forgot. The doors are all locked. Hold on a second.' He hurried back outside, and saw Haldemann and Edwards just going into the theatre. He shouted, and they waited while he trotted across the gravel to them. He said, 'Bob, have you got a general key? One for all the interior doors?'

Edwards said, 'You're making a search? What are you looking for?'

'Not yet,' Sondgard told him. 'Don't worry, I'll keep my side of the bargain. Have you, Bob?'

'Yes, sure. In the office. Come on.'

They went into the theatre, and Haldemann produced a skeleton key from his desk drawer. Sondgard brought it back to the house and he and Mike went upstairs to start searching. Larry Temple was sitting on the bottom stair, his eyes half closed.

After Sondgard/Chax left the room, they all started talking at once, all of them except the madman. He sat slumped in a folding chair, chewing on the inside of his cheek, trying to think.

He had a lot to think about. Sondgard/Chax was closing in on him. Sondgard/Chax was attacking him from everywhere, was giving him too many things to guard against at once.

The search. That was something to think about. He pictured his room upstairs, trying to see if there was anything in it that would help Sondgard/Chax.

Not the furniture. None of that was his, it all came with the room, it was all there when he'd moved in the day before yesterday.

Not the clothing or the suitcase. All of that belonged to the driver he'd killed; none of it could be traced back to Robert Ellington.

And what else was there in the room? Nothing.

Yes, one more thing. His copy of the play they should be rehearsing, with his speeches underlined. But that couldn't be of any help either.

There was the clothing he'd worn last night. The shoes were still wet, for instance. But they were on the floor in the closet, and he had fresh dry shoes on now, and there was no reason to expect Sondgard/Chax to pick those shoes up. He would just open the closet and look in and see clothing hanging from the bar, and shoes on the floor, and that would be all. No reason to touch the shoes at all.

And even if he did, what of it? His shoes were wet. He could think of a story to cover that. He had – He had –

He had taken a shower. Last night he'd come home drunk with the others, and instead of going straight to bed he'd taken a quick shower, but he'd been so drunk he'd stepped under the water without taking his clothes off first. Then he'd taken them all off. It was as simple as that.

That would cover the rest of the clothing, too. The shirt and underwear and socks stuffed still damp into his laundry bag. The damp trousers hanging way back in the corner of the closet. None of the clothing had any obvious bloodstains, so they would have to accept his explanation. And there were plenty of people to testify that they'd all drunk too much last night.

So much for the search. There was nothing to find but some wet clothes, and Sondgard/Chax probably wouldn't even notice them, and even if he did the madman had a sensible explanation for them, so the search wouldn't be so terrible after all. Sondgard/Chax would just be wasting his time and his energy, that's all.

But then there was the fingerprint. Now *that* wasn't clever. He hadn't thought about fingerprints at all, either time. Of course, Sondgard/Chax had admitted there was a chance the fingerprint wouldn't be any good, but it was a small chance.

The business about the fingerprint was stupid. It was not clever. Not in any way. There hadn't been any reason to write that note on the mirror; at this point he could hardly remember why he had wanted to do it at the time. And it had just been foolish not to remember fingerprints. There were so many things he'd forgotten, that he had once known, long ago, before the asylum. He had to be so careful, while he was relearning.

But what to do about the fingerprint? Surely they were watching the house, so it wouldn't be either clever or safe to try to run away now. If there was any way to change his fingerprints between now and three o'clock this afternoon, he didn't know about it.

A nine-to-one chance. That's what Sondgard/Chax had said.

But was that right? Maybe it wasn't a nine-to-one chance. Maybe it was a *one*-to-one chance. Maybe Sondgard was just *hoping* the fingerprint would be good, and was trying to bluff the madman into running away.

Why else would he be searching? If he had a nine-to-one chance, would he waste so much time and energy searching?

He'd admitted, *admitted*, that they couldn't be sure about the fingerprint until they got the enlargement. So how did he know it was a nine-to-one chance?

It didn't matter. The only thing to do was hope. Hope Sondgard/Chax had the odds wrong, and then hope the odds turned out not to favour all the Doctors Chax. It was the only way to handle this threat; wait to see if it turned out to be a real threat. Make no move at all before three o'clock. But if the men from the state capital did come at three o'clock, and did start taking everybody's fingerprints, then that would mean the enlargement had turned out good, and then the madman would see to it that he escaped before his own fingerprints were taken. There would be a lot of milling around when the state men came, a lot of inevitable confusion. He could go out a side window, from the second floor, land on the dirt below, and get away.

So that took care of the second. The search, no real problem. The fingerprint, wait and see. But there still remained a third thing to think about, and that was the most dangerous of all.

Bobby did it.

Who had written that? Who had come downstairs after he had gone to bed, and written that in the jam he'd smeared on the table? Who in this group knew his secrets? Somebody, *somebody*. Somebody knew he was the one who had killed them; and somebody the same somebody the same sneaking somebody somebody knew his real name!

Was it possible? He didn't know *any* of these people, he'd never met any of them before Wednesday, so how could one of them know so much about him?

He hadn't written those words himself, he *couldn't* have. He thought back to last night, and he could remember two times when he'd made aimless lines, scratched lines with his fingers, but he hadn't been *writing* anything, not either time. Once was by the lake, just before he'd washed off the blood. And the other time was in the kitchen, after he'd smeared jam on the table. But he hadn't *written* anything. There wasn't any *reason* to.

(He didn't ask himself why he'd smeared jam on the table; he didn't think about that part of it at all.)

Somebody knew. That was the only answer. Somehow, some way, somebody knew.

But why do such a senseless thing? Either *tell* Sondgard/ Chax, or keep it quiet; but don't just *hint*. What was the purpose?

To scare him? Could someone *else* be the agent of Doctor Chax, someone else instead of Sondgard? Could that be how it was done? And this was simply another of those meaningless and futile tests: Draw a picture of a man and a woman. What does this black blob look like? When I say a word, you say the next word that comes into your head. Read this story and then tell me about it: (A cowboy went to town and bought a city-type suit. His dog refused to recognize him, and actually tried to attack him, until he took off the suit and put his normal clothing back on.) 'There was a cowboy, and a great big dog like a wolf, and he was named Wolf, and the cowboy and Wolf went downtown to the department store where they had the

Santa Claus in the window that nodded his head and waved his hand . . . ' And all at once it was a story about a dog that attacked a mechanical Santa Claus.

But why hadn't Sondgard/Chax said anything about the other killing, the one last night? Was he trying to be clever again, was this more cleverness? They must have found him by now.

Even in the threats he *didn't* make, Sondgard/Chax was dangerous.

If Sondgard *was* the agent of Doctor Chax. But that wouldn't explain *Bobby did it*. And the only explanation of *Bobby did it* was that there really was an agent of Doctor Chax somewhere close, watching him all the time.

Sondgard closing in, narrowing in on him all the time. And now someone else, silent, watching him.

Who? How could he deal with Sondgard if he had to keep thinking about this somebody else? He had to find out who it was.

He looked at the faces. Ralph Schoen? The man had a vicious face, cruel enough certainly to be one of *them*. But he would be too direct, he wouldn't be the type to tantalize this way. Not Schoen.

Not Alden March; too weak, and also too likely a candidate to be opposed to Doctor Chax rather than allied with him.

Not Arnie Kapow or Perry Kent; both were too obviously what they were, and nothing more.

Tom Burns? No, too cynical; Doctor Chax and his agents were all smugly and pompously sincere, sans any kind of humour.

An actor, then? The madman studied the faces, and his gaze came to rest on Mel Daniels.

Mel Daniels.

He was very young, yes, younger than the madman himself, but did that mean anything? They might have chosen someone so young purposely to allay his suspicions.

Mel Daniels had come here a full day late, as though they hadn't known this was where to send him until after the madman had arrived here himself.

And it was Mel Daniels who '*discovered*' the body of Cissie Walker.

Yes! Yes! And it was Mel Daniels who 'discovered' the writing on the kitchen table!

After writing it himself!

It all fitted. Arriving late, 'happening' to discover everything important. The madman nodded to himself, remembering last night; Daniels had stared at him while they were both with the group at the Lounge. Daniels had prodded him, asking questions about the false background, straining his memory of all that the dead actor had told him.

Daniels had been *toying* with him! Testing his 'reactions,' the way they did, the dirty beasts! And testing his reaction again this morning, with this broad hint, this *Bobby did it*, this underhanded taunting.

So it was *Daniels* who had to be taken care of, Daniels and not Sondgard who was in direct league with Doctor Chax.

Well, both had to go. Daniels/Chax, because of what he had done and what he yet might do, and Sondgard, because he was coming too close.

And the sooner the better.

Karen Leacock, the skinny one, came to the door to tell them breakfast was ready. They all went to the room next to the kitchen where the long table was – the regular kitchen table, where the message had been 'found,' wasn't big enough for all of them at once – and the madman joined them there. He had made some discoveries while thinking things through, and he had come to some decisions. As a result, his appetite was very good. He took four pancakes for a starter, and set to.

Sondgard came in a few minutes after the rest of them had started, and sat down at the place they'd left for him, midway down the table, on the other side from the madman. From Sondgard's tight and tired look, the madman knew he'd found nothing. Not even the wet clothing. The madman watched his persecutor – his *two* persecutors – watched them closely and covertly while he himself finished his first four pancakes and forked three more on to his plate.

Sondgard was eating slowly, grimly, plodding through the

breakfast, just mechanically shovelling the food into his mouth at slow and regular intervals. His expression was dour; it was obvious he had no taste for the meal, but was trying in vain to put on a good show.

The madman was pleased. Sondgard *had* been bluffing about the fingerprint. The chances weren't ninety-ten at all. They were probably fifty-fifty, maybe even worse. Otherwise, the failure of the search wouldn't have depressed the policeman so much.

But Daniels, now Daniels. Daniels was eating with gusto, swilling cup after cup of coffee, eating his pancakes even faster than the madman himself, and all the while talking to Mary Ann McKendrick, sitting next to him on the right. Daniels waved his knife and fork around as he talked, and Mary Ann McKendrick laughed sometimes at the things he was saying, and once she looked over at the madman, laughing the while, and all at once the madman understood.

She was laughing at *him*!

Daniels was *telling* her about him! About the 'experiment', the 'research', and all about his fascinating 'reactions'.

The madman clutched his knife and fork, and the food in his mouth turned to wet grey cardboard. He controlled himself with effort, forced himself to remain in his seat, kept himself from lunging across the table at them to slit both their throats. But that would be stupid, that would be the sort of stupid thing he had allowed himself to do before he'd been sent to the asylum. It was because he had followed his impulses regardless of the consequences that he had wound up in the asylum in the first place. He had learned since then, and he was determined to profit by his learning.

Do not follow your impulses regardless of the consequences. Wait.

Follow your impulses only when you can be sure *there will be no consequences*.

Plan.

Act.

Always follow your impulses; do not let them make you be untrue to yourself.

But be clever.

So this was not the time. He couldn't take care of them now, no matter how much he felt the need, no matter how harshly the girl's idiot laughter grated on his ears, no matter how vicious were Mel Daniels' whispered comments about him.

And to think that once he had wanted to befriend that girl!

His attention was distracted from Daniels/Chax and the girl by a conversation that had begun at the other end of the table. Arnie Kapow had asked Sondgard something – whether the killer had to necessarily be one of the people present – and Sondgard was answering. 'There isn't any doubt any more, Arnie. Not after last night. The house was locked up tight. That message on the table had to be left by somebody living here.'

Tom Burns said, 'I thought you said maybe somebody else did it, not the killer. Somebody who knows something.'

'That's possible,' Sondgard admitted. 'But I don't think it's probable.'

I could tell you, the madman thought to himself. You'd be surprised. Daniels/Chax wrote it. The madman felt the urge strong within himself to blurt that out, to see the expressions on all their faces when he told them what he knew and why he could know it, but he held the urge in check, recognizing it for what it was. It was the destructive urge, the same urge that makes a man looking out a high window or over the railing of a tall bridge suddenly want to jump off. The urge was his enemy, not a part of his true self, and so could be and should be ignored.

Still, he had to say something. The urge was that strong in him. He searched for something safe to say and finally said, 'But wouldn't he have run away by now?'

Sondgard turned his head and looked at him. He turns his head, thought the madman, like a snake going to strike. His eyes are cold, blue flecked with grey. His face is bony. I think he is Death.

Sondgard said, 'I don't think he would. He thinks he's safe, because we haven't caught up with him yet.'

Ralph Schoen took over the conversation. 'He'll try now, won't he? He's got to get away before that fingerprint gets here.'

Sondgard's death's-head turned again. 'He may try,' he said.

'On the other hand, I said there was a small chance the print won't be any good, and he may decide to take the gamble, and stick around. I hope he does. I wouldn't want him running around loose. But if he does take the chance, if he does stay, I'm pretty sure we'll have this whole thing wrapped up this afternoon.'

Sondgard's voice was deep, but with faint treble overtones in it, like some announcers on the radio. Some of the Doctors Chax had had voices like that, and faces like that.

Breakfast was ending. They were still asking Sondgard questions, and he was still answering each in the same slow careful manner, his thin bony head turning to face each new questioner, his grey-flecked eyes studying each face with solemn care.

He is dangerous, thought the madman. I must deal with him, too. First, Daniels/Chax and his bitch. Second, Sondgard.

Then all at once Daniels spoke up. He said, 'Captain Sondgard, is it all right for Mary Ann and I to take off for a while?'

Sondgard didn't like the question, the madman could tell. He hesitated, and finally he nodded and said, 'All right. Where are you going, into town?'

'No, for a boat ride.'

'All right. But – ' His head moved, and he gazed generally at the others. 'But,' he said, 'if anyone else wants permission to leave the house for a while, please don't ask me here. I'll stay here awhile; you can come ask me privately.'

He doesn't want to refuse me in front of everyone, the madman thought. Does that mean he knows, after all?

And now Daniels was going out of the house, out of reach. The *coward*! He must know that he'd been seen through, that the madman was on to him. And now he must be afraid, he must be terrified, as always they grew terrified once it was too late. So he was taking the idiot girl, and he was fleeing the house.

And Sondgard was letting him! Didn't *that* prove they were in league?

The madman felt confusion growing within him, like fog creeping up through a crack in a wood floor. Who were his enemies, which of these people, and how many of them? And how much did they know, and to what degree were they in league with one another?

Was Daniels *really* the agent, or was it someone else, someone he hadn't even thought of?

Did Sondgard know the truth, and was he holding off to accommodate the experiment of Doctor Chax? Or was he actually at a loss, waiting for a fingerprint that might not be any good to him at all?

Were Sondgard and Daniels working together, or did Sondgard have no connexion with Doctor Chax at all, or was he working in combination with an agent of Doctor Chax who was not Daniels and whom the madman had not yet uncovered?

There were too many questions, too many uncertainties. Sondgard had said nothing about the second killing; he might have discovered the wet clothing and be saying nothing about that. There was no way to guess whether the fingerprint would be a danger or not. There was no way to be sure how much Daniels/Chax had told Mary Ann McKendrick, or if he had really told her anything at all, or if he had already told other people.

Doctor Chax himself could be outside the house right now, this very minute, watching through a television set, waiting for the conclusion of the experiment. They had one-way windows at the asylum, there was no secret about that. But for here it would probably be closed-circuit television, with the tiny cameras hidden in light fixtures or inside the walls.

The madman looked up at the ceiling fixture, centred over the table, and wondered: Am I looking into the eyes of Doctor Chax? Is he looking down at me right now, and smiling?

Too many uncertainties, too many uncertainties.

Within him, that being, that creature, that *thing* was stirring again. The one who had taken him over and killed the man with the flashlight. The one of whom he had faint and distant earlier memories. He was moving again, right now, stirring, rising, reaching out as though to take control.

The madman fidgeted, frightened. He couldn't lose control now, this mindless being within him would give the whole game away, would be obvious and blatant and stupid. There was no cleverness in it, no thought beyond the rage of the moment. The madman couldn't lose control now without losing everything.

Only till three o'clock, he thought. I have to keep control until three o'clock. Then I'll find out about the fingerprint, and I'll know what to do next, and the being will settle back down again. But I've got to hold on until three o'clock, or I'm going to do something.

Something.

It was a very ugly rowboat. Old, to begin with, and then painted by someone with more paint than sense. White paint had been slopped on, inside and out, thick and lumpy, reminding Mel of the woodwork in old and run-down Manhattan apartments, with layer after layer of paint on them, all mottled and bumpy. This rowboat was like that, in white that gleamed blindingly in the sun.

And red. The nut who'd painted this boat had possessed a can of red paint, too, and this was a nut who would let nothing go to waste. So the boat had been painted white all over, in thick globs and chunks of paint, and then *over* the white there had been smeared two or three layers of red trim. The top edge of the boat's sides was painted red. The seats were painted red. The oars had been dipped in red paint.

It was a very ugly rowboat. But it was the only one they had.

'It belonged to the people who used to own the house and barn,' Mary Ann explained. 'We sort of inherited it.'

'I didn't think you'd own it on purpose.'

'It floats, that's the important part.'

They were standing on a short narrow wooden pier, jutting out over the water from the very edge of the Black Lake Lounge property. Behind them was the blacktop Lounge parking lot, extending away to the left, and some scrubby field going off to the right to meet the nearest stand of trees. Beyond parking lot and field wound the road, and across the road stood the sparkling theatre and the mouldering house.

A sudden idea came to Mel, and he voiced it: 'They painted the boat with what they had left over from the house.'

'*I* did.'

'You did?'

She looked down at the boat with a fond sad smile. 'It isn't a very good job, is it?'

'You should have painted the house instead.'

'It is kind of ugly, isn't it?' She turned and looked back at the house. 'Somehow, it looks uglier now than it used to. It looks more like a haunted house, now.'

'It is. Climb in.'

He held her arm as she stepped down carefully into the boat, then handed her the bag with the lunch they'd packed before leaving. She put it down – the bottom *was* dry – and then sat down on the aft seat. Mel untied the line, dropped it in the boat, and climbed down to sit between the oars. He pushed the boat away from the pier, and Mary Ann, looking past his shoulder toward the house, said, 'Bob meant to have the house painted this year. He hoped to make enough money to do it. Now maybe we won't have a season at all.'

'What about Sondgard and his fingerprint?'

She shook her head. 'I think he's bluffing,' she said. 'Don't you?'

'I hope not. But I did get the same idea, yes.'

'Can you imagine if this just went on and on? All summer long. We couldn't work, we couldn't put on any shows, but nobody would be allowed to leave. All summer long, just sitting around in that gloomy house there, with nothing to do and nowhere to go.'

'Yeah, fine. Let's talk about something else. If you want to talk about the house, how come it's there at all? This is supposed to be a real ritzy neighbourhood.'

'I know.' She smiled again, more girlishly this time. 'That was the old Eggstrom place. For years and years it was just like an eyesore.'

'It still is.'

'You should have seen it when I was a little girl, before the Eggstroms gave it up. The barn looked worse than the house, then. And they had junk all over the yard, every which way. People kept getting up petitions against them and everything.'

'How come they managed to move in there in the first place?'

'Well, they were there first. When they came here, there wasn't anything at the lake at all. The town down at the other end, of course, but that's all. That house is over fifty years old.'

'Doesn't look a day under two hundred.'

'That was the first house ever built out at this end of the lake. Circle North there used to be a dirt road, and it was called Eggstrom Road, because the only place it went was the Eggstrom farm. Then, when all the estates went up, a lot of people wanted to buy the farm, just to tear down the house and barn, but the Eggstroms wouldn't sell. Then, when the old man died, his son sold it to Bob, and he started the theatre. Now the house isn't an eyesore any more, it's just quaint.'

'That'll be the day. Where am I rowing, anyway?'

'Anywhere you want. This was your idea.'

He looked over his shoulder. 'There's an island out there. Is that private property?'

'No, nobody owns that. Nobody lives there or anything.'

'Why not? These estate people go for privacy, with all the fences and everything, they ought to go nuts over an island.'

'It's too small, I think, and most of it is pretty marshy. And when we have a storm I don't think anybody'd want to be out on that island.'

Mel looked up at the sky, but the good weather was still with them, with no sign of a break. The sun was all alone in a pale blue sky.

He didn't row hard. He was in no particular hurry to get to the island, or anywhere else. His whole purpose was to be alone with this girl, and that purpose had already been gained. At breakfast this morning they had started to talk together for the first time as friends, the ice having been broken by the combination of Mary Ann's confession to him of her secret desire and their having shared this morning's discovery together. In the breakfast table conversation the normal interest he already had in her as an attractive female was heightened, and he'd cast around for a suitable excuse to get off in a corner somewhere with her, finally coming up with the idea of their getting a boat and going for a row on the lake. Was there a boat they could use? He'd asked her, and she said as a matter of fact the theatre itself had a boat, a little rowboat, which any member of the company could use. And would she like to go for a boat ride, seeing it was such a beautiful day outside, and etc., and they could use a change of pace from the gloom and doom indoors, and she could be his guide to whatever natural wonders the lake had to offer, and so on and so on. She would, she said, be delighted.

Now his only question was – which was paramount in her mind, to be away from the house or with him? The question loomed large in his mind, but he didn't ask it.

The day really was beautiful, away from the shadow of the house. The pale blue sky above, the darker blue of the lake water all around them, the rich green of the tailored forest surrounding the lake, the darker green of the mountains all around this shallow valley and the darker, fainter tones of the mountains farther away, blending toward a misty purple at the horizon.

A long distance away across the smooth water, toward the town end of the lake, were a number of small sailboats, cats, with vari-coloured sails. One with a bright orange sail crossed in front of one with a bright purple sail, making a moment of garish beauty. Other cats way across the water there had red sails and blue sails and yellow sails, while two sloops, stately by comparison, wore sails discreetly white. The bright hues of the cats on the dark blue water, framed by the dark green of the shore to left and right, made him think of a pool table, with the balls scattered in a random pattern. This was a similar beauty.

He expressed the comparison, and Mary Ann didn't get it at all. 'A *pool* table?'

'Sure,' he said. The oars were at rest for a moment, the little boat bobbing gently on the water. Mel shaded his eyes with his hand and gazed down toward the cats. 'Just like a pool table,' he said.

'For heaven's sake,' she said. 'A *pool* table. You have a real knack for the poetic image.'

'You've just never looked at pool tables,' he told her, irritated because his estimation of her had dropped, and he was afraid this outing with her was doomed to failure.

'Now, be honest, Mel,' she said. 'Have you ever, even once in your life, looked at a pool table and said to yourself, "That reminds me of a lake"?'

'Well, of course not, I never saw anything like – '

'It isn't even the right *colour*. Pool tables are *green*, and this lake is *blue*.'

'Just forget it,' he said. 'Never mind, just forget it.'

'And besides, pool tables are covered with *smoke*, and they don't – ' She stopped abruptly, and clapped her hand to her mouth, and her eyes widened. She stared at him that way for a few seconds, while he wondered what disaster had just struck, and then slowly she lowered her hand from her mouth, shook her head, and said, 'I'm sorry, Mel. I really am.'

'Well . . . sure. That's okay.'

'I *always* do that, *always*. My brother calls me Lucy, Miss Busybody of the Year. You know, from *Peanuts*?'

He found himself grinning, as the irritation faded away. 'So it doesn't look like a pool table,' he said. 'Maybe that's exclusively a masculine image or something.'

'No, I knew what you meant, with the different-coloured sails and all, it's just I always *do* that. I get so *bossy* sometimes, and *picky*.'

'It's the director in you.'

She smiled wanly. 'Maybe it is.'

'Tell me something,' he said, because it was time to change the subject away from pool tables.

'All right, what?'

'When are you going to New York?'

'Oh. I don't know, Mel. Sometime.'

'Why not go this fall? Right after the season ends.'

'If there is a season.'

'Forget that for a minute. This fall. Right?'

'I don't know, Mel.'

'Announce it,' he told her. 'Maybe not yet, while this other thing is hanging over everybody's head, but after it's all straightened away and we get down to being a summer theatre for a change. Tell everybody, the whole company. Tell them, "I'm going to New York this fall. If you can get me some introductions, or find me work some place, I'd sure appreciate it." Do that, will you?'

She frowned, and chewed on her lower lip, and gazed down at the water rippling past the side of the boat. 'I don't know, Mel,' she said.

'If you announce it now, you'll *have* to go.'

'I know.'

'And these people will help you, if they can. I wish *I* could help you. I mean it, I do. But look at me, I mean, I'm just starting out, too. I could use some contacts myself.'

She looked up at him and smiled again. 'It takes courage to do what you're doing,' she said. 'To go away from home, and start from the very beginning. I'm not sure I could do it.'

'You think it over.'

'I will.'

He unshipped the oars and started rowing again, then looked over his shoulder. 'Where is that damn island, anyway?'

'Straight ahead. I'll steer you.'

'Okay.' He looked back the way he had come, past Mary Ann. 'You can't even see the theatre any more,' he said. 'Or the house.'

She twisted around in the seat to look in that direction. 'I'm glad,' she said.

'Same here.' He pulled on the oars, then angled them out of the water and held them high and dripping. 'I'll make you a deal,' he said.

'What?'

'Out of sight, out of mind. For the rest of the day there isn't any theatre any more, and there isn't any house, and there isn't any maniac.'

'Wonderful,' she said.

They smiled at each other, and Mel rowed them toward the island.

After breakfast, Sondgard went to work to deploy his forces, just in case the killer did fall for the bluff and try to get away before three o'clock. He was pretty sure now that the bluff wasn't going to work; the qualification he'd made about its not being one hundred per cent sure it was a good print had been enough to remove the sting. But he hadn't had any choice. He'd *had* to leave himself an out, because by God he *didn't* have a fingerprint. But in covering himself he had drained the effectiveness of the scheme, so it had been a waste of time to start it in the first place.

And Arnie Kapow hadn't helped matters any, asking him at the breakfast table if he expected the madman to try to escape. Answer yes, and he would confirm the madman's belief that all escape routes were closed, and it would be best to stick around and see if the fingerprint was a threat or not. Answer no, and make the bluff obvious to everyone in the county. So he had tried answering yes and no simultaneously, but he had little hope that *that* would work.

Still, there remained the chance – slim though it might be – that the killer *would* try to escape. Sondgard had to work within that possibility, and so he had to see to it that all avenues of escape were blocked, while at the same time he wanted it to appear that one or more exits were *not* blocked.

He was going to have trouble. To begin with, he didn't have enough men. Including himself, the Cartier Isle Police Department boasted a full complement of four men. One of them, Larry Temple, was dead on his feet, and would have to be relieved and taken home before he fell over, and that left three. Even if all other police business – that is, traffic control and general alertness – were ignored, he still had only three men, including himself. And the house, like most houses, had four sides. Right off the bat, he was one man shy.

In addition, he himself had other things to do, and couldn't cut his movements by giving himself guard duty. So that further reduced his forces by two.

There was, of course, always Captain Garrett. Captain Garrett had so many men he didn't know them all by name. Captain Garrett could cordon the house, bring up searchlights and megaphones, grill the suspects, search for clues –

No. There were too many reasons not to call in Captain Garrett at this point, and not the least of them was that Sondgard would be embarrassed to describe his little attempt at bluff to Captain Garrett until after he knew whether it was was going to work or not. Once the killer was captured, Sondgard would be able to tell Captain Garrett the whole story, but not yet. His mistakes and blunders and hesitations would have lost their bite then, when the killer was safely behind bars. Right now they loomed too large; Sondgard wanted no professional on the scene to disparage him.

He told himself he should rise above personal feelings, that he should act out of logic rather than out of emotion, but he just couldn't do it. The argument that this was a case for a humanist rather than a detective had grown pretty threadbare by now; Sondgard was supported now only by a grim tenacity, a determination not to be made an utter fool of.

So he was dependent upon himself, and the forces under his command, which consisted of an ex-Marine who preferred his uniform to his job, a twenty-year-old college student long overdue for sleep, and a man who hadn't thought about anything but boats for the last twenty years.

And, of course, a houseful of interested participants, fourteen of whom were surely his willing allies, with only one adversary against the whole crowd of them.

He would do what he could with what he had. Some other day, he could think it all out and find out what he should have done.

He spoke first to Loueen Campbell, who had her own car, that white Continental convertible parked out in front of the theatre. He asked her if she would do him the favour of driving Larry Temple home, since neither Sondgard nor Mike Tompkins could spare the time to do it.

'I'll be glad to,' she said, and smiled her rather hard and brassy smile. 'If you'll do me a little favour back.'

'If I can.'

'Let me stay in town awhile and do some shopping.' The smile grew satiric. 'Until shortly after three o'clock, say?'

Sondgard smiled back, though he had to force himself a little. 'Fine,' he said. 'Your time is your own.'

'Bless you, Eric.'

Loueen left, taking with her a Larry Temple now more asleep than awake, and Sondgard next phoned the office and talked to Joyce. 'Can you get hold of Dave?'

'I told him what you said before, about staying off his boat and near a phone. He promised to stay right there at home.'

'Fine. Call him and tell him to come on out here, but not to wear the uniform. He should park in front of the theatre, and wait. Sooner or later I'll see him there and come out and talk to him.'

'All right. Will do.'

But Sondgard's mind was still working, editing and correcting his plans even as he implemented them. 'No, wait,' he said. 'I *won't* come out. He's to park in front of the theatre, where he can see both the front and the right side of the house. He's just to sit there, and watch the house. If anyone leaves the house, I'll go out on the front porch with him, with whoever's leaving. If anyone goes out of the house without me escorting him as far as the porch, Dave should honk his horn three times, and keep the guy from getting away. And he should be careful because it may be somebody who's already killed twice.'

'All right, I've got it. How are you doing, Eric?'

'Miserably.'

'Would an expression of confidence from this end do anything for you?'

'It would if I didn't know you were a prejudiced witness.'

'Now, that's what I call egotistical. Phone me when you get him, Eric.'

162

'Will do.'

Next, Bob Haldemann. Sondgard took him to one side and said, 'I want to talk to you privately a minute, Bob.'

'In my room. Come on.'

Haldemann's room was on the first floor, across from the rehearsal room. Sondgard sat in the room's lone chair, and Haldemann sat on the edge of the bed. The shades were drawn and the bed unmade, giving the faint impression that this was somehow a sickroom.

Sondgard said, 'I have news for you, Bob, and I also have favours to ask of you.'

'Anything, Eric, anything at all.'

'Fine. The news first. Number one, our madman didn't just write that message in the kitchen last night. He did other things as well. I'm pretty sure the message doesn't refer to the killing of Cissie Walker at all, but to the second killing.'

'*Second* killing?'

'You know the Lowndes place. Somebody climbed over the gate there last night and beat one of the guards to death.'

'Eric!'

'Wait a second, there's more. Then he went down to the lake, right next to the Lowndes house, and scrawled the name Robert in the dirt three times. Then he turned around and came home. He didn't enter the house, he didn't do *anything* else. All he did was climb over the gate, kill a man, write his name three times, and go home.'

'Robert,' said Haldemann thoughtfully. 'And in the message here, he wrote Bobby. Is he trying to pin it on me, Eric?'

'I don't think so. It wouldn't stick, and he'd have to know that. We're up against a lunatic, Bob, and that's what makes it so tough. There's no figuring out *what* he means, or *why* he does anything. I keep having the feeling that if I could only understand *why* he climbed over that gate in the first place I'd be a lot closer to him than I am now.'

'But you are close, aren't you? At three o'clock – '

'That's the rest of my news. There isn't any fingerprint.'

Haldemann blinked in confusion. 'There what?'

'There was a fingerprint, or there may have been, we're not

163

sure. But we never got a picture of it. Mike bobbled it. It wasn't his fault, just one of those things that could happen to anybody. I'm bluffing, Bob. I'm trying to scare our killer into making a break for it.'

'What if it doesn't work?' Haldemann had paled considerably; obviously the bluff had worked with him, and he was now feeling lost without the comforting reassurance of that fingerprint. If only the killer was believing it as thoroughly.

'I'll worry about that at three o'clock,' Sondgard told him. He leaned back in the chair. 'Both these pieces of news,' he said, 'are confidential for the moment. The fingerprint, obviously. And the second killing, because you and Mike and I are the only ones in this house who know anything about it, except the killer himself. I may be able to use that, though I admit I don't know how.'

Haldemann nodded. His fingers were rubbing together with a dry sound. He said, 'And then there was a favour.'

'Yes. I'm having the house covered on the outside, but I want to avoid any more trouble on the inside. I want you, and two or three of the others, to help me keep an eye on our suspects.'

'Of course.'

'I've got it limited to four. Now, I don't want our killer to believe it's *impossible* to get out of this house, so I wouldn't want somebody following each suspect everywhere he goes. But just to keep an eye on the doors, and the staircases, and the stairs to the basement. If you see somebody in the process of sneaking out, don't try to stop him, just come tell me. I want as early a warning as possible, and Mike and Dave won't know he's on his way till he's already out of the house.'

'All right, Eric.'

'Arnie could help us. And Perry Kent.'

'Ralph?'

'I'd like Ralph to put on a game of business as usual. Start a rehearsal.'

'All right. What about Tom Burns?'

'He's one of my suspects.'

'Tom? For heaven's sake, Eric!'

'I'm going strictly by my timetable, Bob, and by everybody's statements. The timetable eliminates you, and the Daniels boy, and Arnie and Perry, and Ralph and Dick and Alden. And the four women are eliminated, of course. That leaves four, and to tell you the truth none of them looks very likely. But Tom Burns is one of the four. He's a heavy drinker, and he has been for years, which means you can't say definitely when he will or will not snap. He had a lech for the Walker girl. The name written on the kitchen table was Bobby, and if Tom is suffering from some sort of Jekyll and Hyde insanity like – '

'That was just a *story*, Eric!'

'*The Three Faces of Eve* wasn't just a story. If Tom had a split personality caused by all the heavy drinking, then the second personality might very well decide to call itself Bobby Burns.'

'That's fantastic. I'm sorry, Eric, but it really is.'

'This is *all* fantastic, Bob. The killings, the messages, all of it. The work of a sick mind. Obviously, whoever he is he's capable of *looking* normal. So it could be any one of the four, and it could just as easily be Tom.'

Haldemann shook his head dubiously. 'I suppose you're right,' he said, 'but I just can't see Tom as a murderer. *Or* a maniac.'

'All right, neither can I. I can't see any of the other three, either. That's Ken Forrest, and Will Henley, and Rod McGee.'

Haldemann gazed at him thoughtfully, digesting the names, and then shook his head. He said, 'And that's all, Eric? Aren't we forgetting somebody?'

'Who?'

'I just can't – Those three boys are all – they're *normal*, Eric. I've talked to all three of them.'

'So have I.'

'If it's one of those four. I don't see how you'll ever catch him. I couldn't conceive of *any* of them doing things like this. It would *show*, Eric, it would *have* to.'

'Obviously, it doesn't.'

'Mm.' Haldemann thought that over, too, and then said, 'It does have to be somebody here, doesn't it? Yes, I know, it does, we've gone over that already.'

'Yes.' Sondgard got to his feet. 'I have more to do,' he said.

'How much do I tell Arnie and Perry?'

'Who the suspects are, that's all.'

'All right.'

'And they're to keep it to themselves.'

'You know them. If either of them says ten words in a week, it's a miracle.'

'I know.'

Sondgard next went to find Mike, who was still watching the front door, and told him to take up a new station behind the house, where he could watch the rear and right side. And if he were to hear Dave Rand honk his horn three times, to come around front on the double. And if he ran into any trouble, to fire one shot, but not to shoot at any *people* without asking a lot of questions first.

It had taken him a while to get things set up, and he had the uneasy feeling that the whole crowd could have snuck out of the house by now, so he next wandered through the house, taking a private head-count, and was relieved to find everyone present and accounted for. He went out on the front porch to wait for Dave Rand to arrive and take over the surveillance out there.

When Dave showed up, Sondgard waved to him and went down off the porch and over to the theatre. But he didn't stop to talk to Dave, but kept on by and went into the theatre.

Harry Edwards, the wire-service stringer, was happily ensconced in Bob Haldemann's office, seated at Bob's desk and talking on the telephone. Three other men helped fill the small office, sitting around on tables and the other chair. From the way they leaped at him the second he came into the room, Sondgard knew they were also reporters. He waved them away, saying, 'Nothing to say. Not yet, not yet.'

He went over to Edwards, who hurriedly finished his conversation and hung up the phone. Sondgard said to him, 'I hope those are collect calls.'

'Well, sure, T P isn't cheap.'

'So *you* say,' said one of the other reporters.

Sondgard cut into the joking before it had a chance to get well started. He said, 'Are these three it so far?'

'The sum total,' said Edwards. 'There'll be more, though.'

'All right. Pass the word. All reporters are to stay here in the theatre. I don't want any of them wandering around outside the house, peeking in windows. I'm having the house watched, and not all my men can tell a suspect from a reporter, so there could be some confusion. A reporter might even get shot by mistake, and then I'd have to make a public apology. So keep them here, right?'

Edwards laughed aloud, saying, 'I like you, Professor. Your word is law.'

'Fine.'

Sondgard left the office and went back out to the sunlight, noticing what he'd missed before, the sign Harry Edwards had stuck to one of the glass doors: *Press Information – Inside, Turn Right.*

Sondgard thanked God for Harry Edwards. He nodded to Dave again, a big red-faced blond man who looked awkward and cumbersome on dry land, and went back into the house to take up the vigil some more.

'What time is it?'

Mel looked at his watch. 'One-thirty,' he said.

Mary Ann looked out pensively over the water. 'An hour and a half,' she said.

'We weren't going to talk about that,' Mel reminded her. He pointed. 'Look out there. Where's the theatre? Can you see it?'

'No.'

'Nothing but pool balls. Look, there goes an orange one, way down there by the Lounge. What's the orange one? Five, isn't it?'

167

'I don't know.' Her voice betrayed her; she was still distracted, thinking of the other.

Mel got to his feet. 'Come on, come on. We were going to explore.'

'All right. I guess we better leave our shoes off.' She turned her back on the lake and looked at their island. 'It get's pretty swampy.'

'What about snakes?'

'Boy, are you the cheerful one.' She smiled at him, regaining her humour, and shook her head. 'No snakes. And no rabbits or squirrels or anything else, either. We've got the place to ourselves, unless some kids come out.'

'Kids come here?'

'Sometimes. I used to come out here sometimes when I was a little girl. There's an old broken-down shed around on the other side, if it's still there. We played house in it, and the boys played war. It was a pillbox, and the ones inside were Japanese and the ones outside were Marines.'

'Let's see this pillbox.'

'I'm not sure it's even there any more. Come on, we'll go around the island first, and then explore the interior later.'

Mel automatically took her hand, and they started off together, making their way along the water's edge. There was no real beach anywhere around the island; the lake water was wearing the island slowly away, so at the point where land met lake there was usually only a sudden drop of a foot or two, and thick mud, and weeds and bushes growing right down to the edge, so they had to move slowly, and keep in a little from the water.

They had taken their time coming out here, floating around on the water till the sun grew too high and too hot, and then they'd found one of the few places where the ground sloped up gradually from the water, with a small clear grassy patch surrounded by the bushes and weeds, and there they'd landed. There were trees close by, gnarled and stunted, but big enough to offer a little shade. They'd sat a long while in this shade, talking amiably and casually together, telling each other anecdotes of their past life, getting to know one another a little better.

Around one o'clock they'd eaten the lunch, and then digested a while, and now at last they were moving again.

Mel was not at all sure of himself. Mary Ann seemed open and honest and friendly, and she had no objection to being here alone with him, but he wasn't at all sure just how much that meant. Because she was gradually assuming more and more importance to him, he wanted to make no rash or ill-advised moves, wanted to avoid inadvertently driving her farther away from himself.

So he hadn't yet kissed her. He'd been thinking about it, more or less constantly, ever since they'd landed here, but as yet he hadn't even begun a move in that direction.

He argued with himself about it, telling himself that after all she *had* come out here with him, and after all under circumstances like this she had to *expect* him to kiss her, didn't she? But God alone knew what went on in the minds of girls; she might not be expecting to be kissed at all. She might be thinking of the two of them now as sister and brother.

On the other hand, what if he *didn't* try to kiss her, and she'd been waiting all day for him to make the first move? Wouldn't that be just as bad? If she did want to be kissed, and he didn't kiss her, wouldn't that drive her away from him just as surely as if she didn't want to be kissed and he did try?

It was a problem.

And, damn it, it wasn't *always* a problem. He'd had his share of girls, by God. Not all of those stories he'd told in the Lounge last night were false. He could make out as well as anybody, all things considered, and since living in New York had more than one night slept in a bed not his own. So why the big problem, all of a sudden?

He thought back to his earlier conquests, as he walked along hand in hand with this problem girl, trying to figure out what he had done those times that he was not doing now, or in what way the girl had been different, or the situation different.

Well, the situation was different enough, with this cloud hanging over everybody's head. But to a certain extent they were out from under that cloud right now, even if only temporarily, and that should help equalize things.

The difference was, when all was said and done, this time he *cared*. He'd known the girl not yet twenty-four hours, but there it was just the same. It's easy to be a make-out artist if you don't give a damn about the girl; just go ahead and try. If she goes along with you, you're in. And if she slaps your face and stalks off in a huff, small loss.

That was the difference. This time, big loss.

He thought about it all the way around the island, which, despite the slowness of their progress, didn't take long. The island was very small, about fifty yards by thirty, and before he knew it they were back where they'd started, with the white-and-red rowboat bobbing at the end of its line, and the orange cat still tacking back and forth way down there by the Lounge.

'That's enough for me for a while,' she said. 'Let's sit down and rest a minute.'

'Fine.'

He sat down next to her, and all of a sudden there was nothing to say. He'd done fine with the small-talk bit up till now – a lot better than anything else – but all of a sudden there weren't any more words. Maybe because of the realization he'd come to on the trek around the perimeter of the island: small loss versus big loss. Whatever the reason, right now he had absolutely nothing left to say.

So he kissed her.

Just like that. Out of desperation, more than anything else; the silence had been getting uncomfortable. For lack of anything better to do, he'd kissed her.

It was a short kiss, and not exactly a ball of fire. Then he sat back a little ways, looking at her, listening to something thudding in his chest, and wondering what her reaction would be.

She smiled. 'I thought you'd never do it,' she said.

Quarter after two, and nothing was happening. Sondgard paced through the house, back and forth, back and forth, from front door to kitchen to front door to kitchen. From behind the closed doors of the rehearsal room came the drone of the rehearsal; Ralph Schoen was in there with Dick Lane and Alden March, who had three scenes alone together. Schoen couldn't work with any of the others, because Loueen Campbell was in so many scenes, and he didn't want to have someone else reading her lines. He had some sort of mystical director's reason for this, having the actual actors present for the early rehearsals, so Sondgard hadn't argued the point. But it left all four of his suspects at loose ends, here and there throughout the house.

In a way, that might be good. The killer would have nothing to distract his mind. He would *have* to think about the three o'clock deadline. He would have time and leisure to worry.

But it was now quarter after two, and still nothing had happened. It was time, Sondgard thought, to apply a little extra pressure. So he broke off his pacing and went in search of his suspects.

He found Tom Burns first, sitting in the dining-room at the long table there, a bottle and glass in front of him. He was drinking slowly but steadily, and he was doodling with a pencil on a sheet of paper, drawing sleek, highly chromed automobiles. He looked up when Sondgard entered, and waved cordially. 'Greeting, Hawkshaw. Get yourself a glass.'

'No thanks.' Two hours ago, they'd all been gathered in this room for lunch, a meal as uneventful as the morning's, but even quieter. There had been no questions for him that second meal. Sighing, he sat down across from Tom and said, 'You know Eddie Cranshaw very long?'

'Eddie who?'

'Cranshaw. You know, the skinny guy with the missing fingers.'

Burns frowned in concentration. As always, his mobile face

exaggerated the expression, making it seem unreal. Or *was* it unreal? It was so hard to tell what a maniac's face would look like.

Burns at last shook his head. 'I don't know the guy at all,' he said. 'Cranshaw? With missing fingers? What a description.'

'You know, Everett Lowndes' friend.'

'Is that the guy owns the place down the road?'

'That's him.'

'I met him once, but I don't know any of his friends. We borrowed a chandelier from him.'

'A what?'

Burns laughed. 'Yeah, doesn't it? A chandelier. Remember, three seasons ago, *The Apple Seed*? That dog of a thing. You saw it, didn't you?'

'It sounds familiar.'

'So it needed a chandelier. The whole family keeps talking about the chandelier, remember?'

Sondgard nodded slowly. 'It's coming back to me,' he said.

'Well, this guy Lowndes had a spare chandelier in his basement, and he loaned it to us. Weighed a ton. We had to borrow Anderson's truck, it wouldn't fit in the wagon.'

'And that's the only time you met Lowndes.'

'I suppose he's come to the shows sometimes, I wouldn't know.'

'That's right.' Sondgard rubbed his palm against his forehead. 'To think,' he said. 'Three murders. I can hardly believe it myself.'

Burns looked startled. '*Three?* I only know about one.'

Sondgard looked at him, blinking in pretended befuddlement. 'Did I say three? I hope to God that wasn't a presentiment.'

'Eric, dear heart, are you trying to be cute with me?'

'I couldn't be cute with anybody right now, Tom. I'm exhausted. I just wish three o'clock would get here.'

'Do you really think *I* might have bumped off poor Miss Cissie Walker?'

'Who knows who did what?' Sondgard got to his feet. 'I'm liable to go take a nap on Bob's bed,' he said. 'I'll see you later.'

172

'Have fun, Hawkshaw.'

As Sondgard went out, Burns poured himself another drink. Would this work? He had no idea; but he was willing to try anything now. He would go through the same routine with each of them, hoping to catch some sort of reaction from the names, or the description of Eddie Cranshaw, or the 'mistake' in the number of murders. Or, at the very least, to rattle the killer a little more, convince him that Sondgard was getting closer.

He went out to the hall and to the stairs and started up, intending to rouse out one of the other three, when he met Ken Forrest coming down. 'Ah, there you are,' he said. 'I've been looking for you.'

'For me?' There was no fear, or guilt, evident in Forrest's eyes. He was, in fact, smiling helpfully, eager to be of assistance.

'I was wondering how long you knew Eddie Cranshaw.'

'Who?' Forrest glanced up the stairwell, as though expecting to find someone named Eddie Cranshaw up there. 'He's not somebody here, is he?'

'No, he's Everett Lowndes' friend. With the missing fingers.'

If Forrest's baffled smile was phoney, he was the most accomplished actor in the building. 'I just don't know what you're talking about,' he said.

'You don't know Everett Lowndes?'

'Well, gee, I don't know, maybe I do.' He scratched his head in a boyish gesture; he seemed more outgoing than he had yesterday, probably because he'd been here longer now and was beginning to loosen up. 'Would I know him from New York?'

'No, I don't think so.' Sondgard returned his smile – he still might be the killer, so the pretence had to be maintained – and said, 'Don't mind me, I'm just tired. Maybe it wasn't you at all that knew Eddie Cranshaw. Maybe it was Rod McGee knew him, and I've got my facts wrong. After three mur –'

But the boy didn't let him finish. He said, 'Are you kidding, Captain Sondgard?' The baffled smile was back on his face, as strong as ever.

Sondgard's brows came together. 'Kidding about what?'

'What do you mean, maybe *Rod McGee* was the one knew him?'

'But – '

Sincerity and bewilderment on his face, Forrest patted his own chest, saying, 'For Pete's sake, Captain Sondgard, *I'm* Rod McGee.'

As soon as he said it, the madman knew he'd made a mistake. For one awful second of vertigo, he was completely lost, swirling down in a whirlpool, as helpless and unknowing as an infant, even losing his balance on the stairs and starting to fall blindly and unknowingly downward . . .

And then it all came rushing back. Who he was. Where he was. How he had come to be here, and what had happened to him here, and what events had let to this last irrevocable blunder.

The being had come over him again, just after lunch. It had been growing and growing all morning, gaining strength from his increasing panic as the three o'clock deadline neared. The conviction had strengthened in him that Daniels knew all, that he was indeed the agent of Doctor Chax, and that Sondgard knew as well, that Doctor Chax had set three o'clock as the time for the end of the experiment, and that at that time they would all swoop down on him at once: the Doctors Chax, Daniels, Sondgard, the state police, the male nurses, everyone, all of them, the whole world.

Until, almost gratefully, he had succumbed, he had abdicated, and the being had taken over, blunt, pragmatic, mindless.

And had become someone else!

Memory surged back into his mind, and understanding, even while comprehension was slowly coming over Sondgard's features, even while Sondgard was stepping back from him, opening his mouth to cry out.

The madman *leaped*!

Batter! Batter! Close the grey-flecked eyes, and run!

He was over the crumpling Sondgard, at the door, out and

away. The hunter's horn sounded, and again, and a third time. Shouts went up. The pack was baying at his heels.

He ran flat out, with total physical effort, straight as an iron rod, and all at once the lake was in front of him again, glinting now in sunlight, and he kept running, white sprays of water crashing out away around his pistoning legs, till he was in too deep to run, the water clung to his legs, and he dove forward into it.

Behind him, the hunter's horn sounded again, and then the flat dead cracks of shooting. Pistols, guns. Bullets.

He dove beneath the surface, hiding away in the cold depths, *pushing*, clawing his way through the water, farther and farther from shore, until his lungs were on fire and he had to surface again.

He didn't look back. He surfaced for one scant instant, long enough to expel the dead and burning air, drag into his lungs the new cold air, see the flash of orange ahead of him, and submerge again.

Toward the flash of orange. Against all the dullness of blue and green, there had been only that one flash of orange. Not questioning it, only accepting and driving forward, thrusting forward, he clawed through the yellow-green water toward where he had seen the flash of orange.

He surfaced again for more air, and it was closer, much closer, and now he could see it was a sail. He was far from shore, close to the tiny boat with the orange sail. He submerged once more.

This time, before he had to surface, he saw undulating ahead and above him the curved bottom of the boat. Clamping his mouth shut against the need to breathe, he scuttled onward, arms and legs flailing and thrashing, under the boat and up at last on the other side.

His hand came up, clutched the side of the boat. The other hand followed. He pulled himself up, and rolled over the rail, and fell on the couple sleeping entwined together, nude and golden on a pale pink blanket.

There was no question, no hesitation. They were struggling up from their sun-sleep, and in a moment they would begin to make noise, and tell the Doctors Chax where their victim hid. He struck the girl with his right fist, twice, hard straight downward slams against her face, and the freshly opened eyes misted and reclosed. His left hand was already on the man's throat, clutching as though to life itself. His other hand came over.

The man thrashed on the bottom of the boat like a giant fish, his hands clawing at the hands around his throat. But the madman clung, and clung, and clung, and slowly the giant fish died.

Then the unconscious girl. She did not awaken, nor struggle. And he felt no carnal desire for her, her nudity meant nothing to him. Since that one time, when everything had gone wrong, those desires had never come back to him at all. He was by now too remote from living things to retain still the instinct of life to renew itself.

Moving carefully, revealing himself over the boat's rail as little as possible, he tilted them up and over, lowering them slowly into the water. The bodies trailed down into the yellow-green darkness, floating downward, arms waving good-bye, the girl's fair hair floating out and up away from her head, streaming down after her in great beauty.

Alone. Safe. In a new haven. The madman looked about himself.

There was a Thermos jug with a plaid exterior, half full. He tasted, and it was sweet lemonade. There was clothing, his and hers, scattered around the bottom of the boat, as though they had undressed in great haste and distraction.

His own clothing was once again sodden. He stripped it all off, threw it all over the side. That clothing would mark him now, as the clothing he had worn in his escape from the asylum would have marked him. No longer could he be Ken Forrest, and the attempt to be Rod McGee had been doomed from the start.

He couldn't let that being take over again. It was dangerous, it couldn't plan, it did stupid and wasteful things.

He tried the man's clothing on, but the shoes were far too small. The trousers fit him at the waist, but were too short in the legs. And the shirt was too small. So he had nothing now but trousers.

He peered over the railing, looking back toward the gleaming red theatre. Was there pursuit? He could see none. But this little boat with its orange sail could not be a haven for long. He had to find a more permanent refuge, at least until tonight. Under cover of darkness he could escpae again. With a new name, and new identification papers. The dead man, according to the papers in his wallet, had been named Frank Marcangelo.

The madman – Frank Marcangelo now – peered over the railing, searching for refuge. The shore was dark and green, but all of it estates, all patrolled by guards with guns and cars.

He saw the island.

Sondgard stood in the doorway, looking at the body of Rod McGee sprawled across the bed. 'All right,' he said. '*All right.*'

There was a cut beneath his right eye, where Ken Forrest had slashed him with his fingernails, trying to gouge his eyes out. There was a heavy pain in the back of his head, where he had hit it on the floor when he was knocked down.

His face was ashen. His eyes were cold, and bleak. His face seemed bonier, thinner than before.

He had let this happen. He had *caused* this to happen. His bluff had worked, had flushed the madman out, but at *this cost*.

All right. This was an end on it. No more. There was a rabid dog loose in the district; he would be cut down like a rabid dog. Cut him down first, pity him afterwards.

Sondgard turned away and hurried downstairs. Mike Tompkins was at the wheel of his pretty car, gunning the engine in impatience. Dave Rand had already gone on ahead, to get the launch ready. Joyce Ravenfield had been telephoned, and had probably already called Captain Garrett. Before sundown, this whole area would be cordoned. There would be searchers everywhere. The rapid dog would no longer have it all his own way, aided and abetted by a blundering stupid egotistical part-time cop.

Sondgard got into the police car, and Mike backed it quickly around in a tight hard circle, and jolted it forward on to the road. He said, 'What'd you find?'

'McGee's dead.'

'Jesus Christ Esquire on a crutch.'

'Shut up and drive.'

Sondgard wasn't happy with Mike Tompkins now. He came close to hating Mike Tompkins now, partly because he was close to hating himself now and therefore was close to hating the whole world, and partly because Mike Tompkins was all bark and no bite. He went away and learned how to take fingerprints, and when he's handed the one fingerprint in his life that's *important*, he mashes it with his big stupid hands. He spends hours every day shooting at targets out on the practice range, and when for once in his life he's shown an *important* target, the bobbing receding head of that rabid dog, he misses. A bragging, fat-head, big-chested, uniformed idiot.

He's almost as bad, thought Sondgard grimly, as I am.

They rode in silence, Mike at least *driving* like a man who knew how. The siren wailed, the car careened around the curves, the red speedometer needle in its trembling never dropped below eighty.

They burst into town, across the stunned intersection at Broad Avenue and on to Circle North, and Mike took the dirt turn-off on two wheels. The car shuddered to a stop at the foot of the pier where Dave Rand already had the launch's engines growling.

It was not a new launch, but Dave kept it painted and shining, the lettering crisp on its cabin. Through local ordinance, it was the only motor-powered craft allowed on this lake. Sondgard and Mike ran out on the pier and jumped on to the launch, and Dave shouted at them from the wheel to loose the lines.

After the mad scramble to get to the launch, the next hour and a half was slow and dragging anticlimax. Dave roared the launch down to the farther end of the lake, where the madman had gone in, and they crossed back and forth, back and forth, searching the shore through binoculars, searching this area of the lake. They didn't concern themselves with the island; it was too far away for a man to have swum it.

At four o'clock, the first state police cars appeared at their end of the lake, and Sondgard through his binoculars saw Captain Garrett standing at the water's edge, near the Lounge, waving to him. He turned to Dave. 'Go on in to shore.'

They couldn't get the launch in to the short pier where the theatre's rowboat had stood, but there was a longer pier behind the Lounge itself. Dave eased the launch in next to it, and Sondgard and Mike threw the lines to two uniformed state policemen, who held them while Captain Garrett came aboard.

He was a bluff and hearty man, invariably cheerful of manner, surrounded by an aura of fantastic patience and competence. He shook Sondgard's hand and said, 'You've got a rough one this time, eh, Eric?'

'Do you want to hear it now?'

'If it'll help.'

Sondgard told it quickly, sketching in what the madman had done, and what he had done in retaliation, outlining his own blunders as clearly as possible. But Captain Garrett immediately reassured him, saying, 'Don't go putting on a hair shirt, Eric. You were up against a lunatic. A normal killer now, somebody who kills for a *reason*, you can almost always track one of those fellows down. But a lunatic now, that's a horse of a different colour. I think you did just fine. You flushed him out in a day, didn't you? Couldn't ask for better than that.'

'Two people died who shouldn't have died.'

'You thinking about that fingerprint? Now, don't go putting a lot of hope in one lone fingerprint off a cake of soap. Just listen to me, I'm making up poems. But take my word for it, Eric, that little slip with the soap could have happened to anybody. And it probably wasn't a print worth a damn anyway. Soap's too soft, it blurs the outlines.'

'Rod McGee is dead,' Sondgard said bitterly.

'That boy would probably of been killed anyway. Him or somebody else. He got killed because you flushed this Forrest fella out. Now, if you hadn't flushed him out, how many people would of been killed? Maybe this same Rod McGee, plus a whole lot more. Don't you go getting mad at yourself, Eric, you did this just fine. I can't think of anything I'd of done different, and there's one or two *excellent* things you did I wouldn't of even thought of.'

Sondgard remained unconvinced, but he let the conversation lapse because they were wasting time. They agreed that Captain Garrett would take charge of the search on shore, and Sondgard would stay on the launch. Forrest had undoubtedly crawled on to land somewhere by now, but he might just try heading back into the water again if Captain Garrett's men got too close to him.

They spent a little while setting up a radio connexion between the launch and one of the state police cars, through the nearest state police substation and Joyce Ravenfield back at the office. Then Captain Garrett left the launch, and they headed out into the lake again.

Four o'clock. Four-fifteen. Four-thirty.

A flash of colour kept itching the corner of Sondgard's eye. A flash of colour, an irritant. He kept trying to concentrate his attention on the shoreline and the near water, and this flash of orange colour kept intruding on him, until all at once his mind was full of it.

Orange. A bright orange sail out beyond the madman's bobbing head, when Mike had been shooting and missing. And now, a bright orange sail . . .

He turned, squinting, peering for it. Down by the island. Stopped there, down by the island.

It didn't have to mean a thing. Somebody out for a sail, and taking a break on the island.

But the madman had disappeared. And that orange sail had been down at this end of the lake before.

Sondgard hesitated. But one more blunder now, and he didn't know what he'd do with himself. He turned to Dave. 'Go on over to the island,' he said. 'Let's just take a look at the island.'

It was a one-room shed, as old as the hills. Half the roof had rotted away, part of one wall had fallen outward, and if there had once been flooring, it was now all gone. The windows were blank rectangles in the standing walls, and there was no door in the doorway.

Mel stepped inside, gazed around, and said, 'Charming.'

'I hoped you'd like it,' she said. 'The servants are off today, so we'll have to rough it.'

'In appointments like this, who could complain?'

They were both feeling very giddy, and completely unaware of the passage of time. They'd spent a long, long while doing a lot of necking and very little talking, and had stopped only when it had become obvious to both of them that within the next minute they must either stop or mate. The spell broken, they were nervously hysterical with one another, laughing too much, touching one another gingerly and trying to make believe that they were all calm inside.

They'd gone swimming again, for the cooling influence of the water, and then had spent a while just lying on the ground, smoking and talking idly. They got around to Mary Ann's future again, and this time she agreed that she probably would go to New York this fall, and he would introduce her to everybody he knew, because who knows, somebody might know of a job for her. They talked it over and decided she should ask Bob Haldemann for some acting jobs in the plays this summer, so she could qualify for Equity membership and then try her hand at acting when she got to the city. She couldn't very well expect to walk into New York and be given a job as a director, but if she could act even fairly decently she might get some work and meet some people, and once again, who knows?

The sun had climbed to the top of the sky and then slid halfway down the other side, so that now it was facing them, shining hot and yellow in their eyes, finally forcing them to move on. 'I still haven't showed you the shed,' she reminded him.

'I'm game,' he said. 'Let's go.'

So they picked their way in through the shrubbery, the ground marshy and oozing beneath their bare feet, and came to the shed. They played a nonsense game here, making it up as they went along, gradually becoming Cynthia and Reginald in an English sentimental comedy, drinking imaginary tea from imaginary cups and telling one another how much they would miss one another while she was being a missionary in Ceylon and he was back with his outfit in Inja.

Then a voice said, 'Doctor Chax.'

They turned, and Mel smiled with surprise. 'Ken! What are you doing here?'

The madman came into the room with a stick.

Chax.

The madman had come to the island. Had crawled from the little boat with the orange sail, had rested awhile on the wet ground, exhausted from the unfamiliar labour of steering a small sailboat across open water, exhausted more from the turmoil raging inside his head.

Chax.

All his beings were active now, all his selves, commingled and confused together. Even the artificial ones, the ones he had assumed with conscious knowledge, for conscious purposes. All mixing together, all babbling at once, all in mortal terror of extinction.

Chax.

The sun beat down, baking his body, drying the sweat that sprang constantly to his burning forehead, covering his eyes with orange haze. Once again – as always and always – he was alone and exposed, the bright light of the sun beating down from above, pointing him out to his enemies, and the flat empty water all around. *All* around this time, encircling him, holding him while his enemies crept closer.

Chax.

Up on his feet, the madman moved. Aimless, directionless, goalless, only driven to move by the knowledge of pursuit and by the thrashing flailing shrieking inside his head. Moving on around the perimeter of the island until he had come to a small grassy spot at the water's edge, and a gleaming white rowboat with red trim bobbing there, floating at the end of a thick rope.

Chax.

On the island. Somewhere on the island. Someone was on this island, and who could that someone be but Chax? He must have a headquarters, he must have a hidden lair, some place from which his orders beamed, some place in which he could watch his television pictures, direct the persecution and the torture and the experimentation on Robert Ellington, Robert Ellington, who had been chosen from all the world as his special victim, the particular guinea pig, the lone opponent.

Chax.

Here he must be, and here the madman would find him. Find him, seek him out, search out the entrance to his underground lair, his burrows and caverns, track him down and smash him once and for all in his own fortifications. And then, with the brain gone, could the limbs go on? The persecution would have to end, the hunters would have to give up their search.

Chax.

The madman groped inward from the water, crawling now on all fours, searching for the entranceway. He came upon a gnarled and stunted tree, and ripped from it a dead branch to use as a club. Then he crawled on, looking for his enemy.

Chax.

At last he heard voices, and knew he had been right. At long last, to succeed, at long last to win through, at long last to be given peace eternal! He moved toward the sounds of the voices, crawling low against the ground, not wanting to give himself away, not wanting the enemy to know how close he had come already, how much closer he would be before long.

Chax.

The structure loomed ahead of him, cleverly camouflaged.

He inched toward it, his streaming face streaked with mud and sweat, his hands and forearms muddy from the crawling, his bare feet brown with mud, the too-small trousers caked with mud.

Chax.

He reached the corner of the structure, edged around it, closer, seeing a window ahead, and inching toward it.

Chax.

And stopped beneath the window, and raised his head, and gazed in upon them there.

Chax.

And saw it was Daniels/Chax, who he had known to be Chax, from the beginning.

Chax.

And moved farther, to the doorway, and straightened, the club gripped in his hand.

Chax.

And entered, speaking his name.

Chax.

And Chax fell away from him, frightened.

Chax.

The tears in his eyes.

Chax.

The fear in the eyes of the woman.

Chax.

And the club was raised.

Chax.

And framed in the window stood Sondgard/Chax, a pistol in his hand.

The madman's head moved, back and forth, and he growled and mumbled in his throat, not knowing which was the head and which only the limb, which to kill to destroy the other.

And Sondgard/Chax in the window said, 'I have only one thing to do right. I have to do just this one thing right. And this is it.'

And the pistol spat oblivion.

Dr Raymond Peterby said, 'Thank you,' and hung up the telephone. His fingertips came together to form a little tent, and he gazed out from the warm small lighted space around his desk, toward the darkness of the darkest corner of the room.

It was night, now. Beyond the draped window, the night was dark, except for the garish brilliance of the spotlights around the maximum-security building. But in here, in this office, there was only the soft light from the desk lamp gleaming on the dark polished wood of the desk top, and soft darkness in all the corners.

We have so far to go, thought Dr Peterby sadly. So much education to do. How little they understand our work, what we are trying to do here. How little they try to help us.

Outside, it is still the Middle Ages, so far as mental science is concerned. The layman looks on the mentally ill and sees only danger and viciousness. He does not see the potential locked up inside that sick mind. He does not see the possibilities for unlocking that potential, healing that sick mind, restoring yet another healthy citizen to the world.

The layman sees only danger, and his only thought is to kill.

They didn't have to kill Robert Ellington. The man had great potential, a brilliant mind, great talents. To waste such a man, to throw him away like rubbish, to sacrifice him to general ignorance, was a crime. Shot down by some ignorant brute, and of the two, the slayer and the slain, which had the greater potential for society?

Dr Peterby noticed the tent he had made of his fingertips, but for once he didn't promptly pull his hands apart. For once, he didn't care. For once, he was happy to admit that yes he *would* like to crawl away from the world and hide. Away from any world that so mistreated as valuable a one of its creatures as Robert Ellington.

Dr Peterby was very sad.

More about Penguins

Penguinews, which appears every month, contains details of all the new books issued by Penguins as they are published. From time to time it is supplemented by *Penguins in Print*, which is a complete list of all books published by Penguins which are in print. (There are well over three thousand of these.)

A specimen copy of *Penguinews* will be sent to you free on request, and you can become a subscriber for the price of the postage. For a year's issues (including the complete lists) please send 4s. if you live in the United Kingdom, or 8s. if you live elsewhere. Just write to Dept EP, Penguin Books Ltd, Harmondsworth, Middlesex, enclosing a cheque or postal order, and your name will be added to the mailing list.

Some other crime and mystery books published by Penguins are described on the following pages.

Note: *Penguinews* and *Penguins in Print* are not available in the U.S.A. or Canada

Michael Innes

Appleby at Allington

Although Sir John Appleby had retired, his detective's instincts and experience hadn't.

When the first body was discovered at Allington Park, he was quite content to believe that it was an accident. But the second body starts him thinking. Two deaths, one after another, is tragic coincidence and Sir John doesn't believe in coincidence.

So he digs around. How did Owain Allington buy back the family estate? Why was he so attached to his rather dissolute nephew, Martin Allington?

In a recent 'Son et Lumière', there had been mention of treasure at Allington Park. But everyone who could gain from it had shrugged it off as pure fiction.

Only some of them had shrugged it off a lot more intensely than others.

Also available:

Not for sale in the U.S.A.

Also by Donald Westlake

Killy

Walter Killy was a tough trade union official who could
tell a 'sewed-up' town in one sniff . . .

Paul Standish was a college boy idealist who thought there
was only one kind of Truth . . .

Together they went to Wittburg and walked slap into a
frame-up for murder . . .

Killing Time

One private eye in his time sees many things
– if not enough to incriminate a whole town, at least enough
to ruin most of its governing officials –
that's why the only private eye in the town of Winston, New
York, was worried when some people who called themselves Citizens for Clean Government started trying to
investigate what was strictly *his* responsibility
– especially since someone had tried to kill him the night
before . . .

Not for sale in the U.S.A. or Canada

Also by Donald Westlake
and now a film by Paramount

The Busy Body

'Digging up a grave, I don't like the whole idea of it.'
'It's a Catholic cemetery, there won't be any evil spirits
around.'

Al Engel was Nick Rovito's right hand – second fiddle
to the biggest gangster in New York. But Al never really
fitted the part – all that killing, kidnapping, pimping,
fixing the unions and peddling dope. Worst of all, he never
saw himself as a grave-robber . . .

and

361

he saw his father murdered . . .

he dedicated his life to revenge . . .

but in the end the avenger with the glass eye faces a
terrible truth . . .

Another Crime and Mystery book by Donald Westlake

The Mercenaries

When Billy-Billy Cantell, a shaky little Lower East Side heroin addict and retailer, wakes up in a strange apartment with a strange murdered woman, he just slips out before the cops arrive.

He's nicely set up to take the rap, with the Homicide boys very hot on his tail. But Ed Ganolese, Master of the Organization (which trades chiefly in drugs, girls and politicians), has special reasons for wanting him preserved. And for dealing with the real killer personally . . .

Not for sale in the U.S.A. or Canada